Austin O'Malley doesn't intend to stay for the wedding reception. He'll watch the service and offer his congratulations before leaving. While he's happy for his friend, he doesn't want to bring down the spirits of the other guests with his dark attitude. Then he plans to head to his mountain retreat and enjoy a secluded vacation that's been a long time coming. He needs the time to come to grips with the deaths of his two middle brothers as well as what he must do next — reach out to his estranged youngest brother with the news of what's happened.

All Austin's plans change when the headiest aroma teases his nostrils while at the wedding. Sitting in the back, he doesn't know where it's coming from, making the ceremony the longest twenty minutes of his life. Afterward, he tracks the smell to a cute little twink with soulful brown eyes. A whispered question to a friend he'd seen talking to the man reveals his name is Pete Saugner, a councilman's private mechanic.

When Austin approaches Pete, he's alarmed by the fear he spots in the much smaller man's eyes. A fellow shifter shares what Pete's scent should have told Austin. His mate is human, although he does know about paranormals. Can Austin figure out how to connect with Pete and keep him safe from a specter from his past?

The Buffalo's Mechanic
Copyright © 2022 Charlie Richards
ISBN: 978-1-4874-3598-1
Cover art by Angela Waters

Published by eXtasy Books Inc

Look for us online at:
www.eXtasybooks.com

THE BUFFALO'S MECHANIC
SHIFTER'S REGIME 10

BY

CHARLIE RICHARDS

DEDICATION

Family — A little bit of crazy, a little bit of loud, and a whole lot of love.
~Unknown

CHAPTER ONE

Sitting on the side of the bed, Austin O'Malley stared at the contact information on his phone. He hovered his thumb over the green call icon. With a huff of frustration, he tapped the sleep button instead.

Austin knew he shouldn't keep putting off calling his youngest brother—Bran. The man had a right to know that their middle brothers—Gaston and Ephram—had been put to death for siding with a rogue ex-councilman. He just couldn't figure out the right words.

How do I tell my estranged brother, a man I haven't spoken to in over fifty years, that our brothers are dead?

Bran had never forgiven Austin for walking away from their water buffalo shifter herd to become a council enforcer. It hadn't mattered that Austin had sent money home to their mother every month until the day she'd died. Bran had held the belief that Austin, as the oldest, should have stayed in their herd to care for her after their father had passed.

Austin hadn't shed a tear when that man had died. He and their mother hadn't been fated mates. Their mating had been arranged by their alpha, and his father hadn't been a nice man. Austin had known if he'd stayed, he would have ended up in the same situation—mated to some woman of the alpha's choosing and urged to pop out several kids to strengthen the herds' numbers.

He'd left as soon as a viable opening appeared.

Having Gaston and Ephram follow in his footsteps, also becoming shifter council enforcers, had been the tipping point.

Bran had stopped returning his letters.

And now, they're dead.

Even though technology changed with the invention of the phone, and Austin had discovered Bran's phone number decades before, he'd never tried calling him.

Will he even answer?

Rubbing his palm over his face, Austin scratched at the edges of his goatee. When he lowered his hand, he glanced at his alarm clock on the nightstand. Heaving a sigh, he rose to his feet.

"Time to get changed," he muttered to himself, placing his phone beside the clock. "Don't want to be late for Dane's wedding."

As Austin changed into a nice pair of black jeans and a navy green polo shirt, his black dress boots completing the outfit, he thought about Dane Drudeson. The Komodo dragon shifter was a fellow council enforcer. While out on a job, he'd met his mate in a small human male, Danny Nunez. After stopping Danny's father from trying to sell him to a slave ring, Dane had popped the question, and Danny had said yes.

Marriage wasn't traditional for shifter couples, but Dane had wanted to do right by Danny in human terms.

Weird, but whatever.

Austin didn't understand it. They were fated mates. Dane had claimed Danny, creating an unbreakable bond between them. Danny would live as long as Dane, and they would be together forever.

What the hell was the point of marriage?

With a shrug of one shoulder, Austin dismissed his thoughts. It wasn't his place to worry about. He would go to the wedding and support his friend. Then he'd start his own vacation.

After sliding his belt through the loops of his jeans, Austin clipped on his phone carrier. He grabbed his phone and slipped it into the holder. Then he picked up his keys in one hand and his duffel bag with the other. He slung the strap over his shoulder so he could carry his hiking boots, too.

Austin didn't plan on returning home for two weeks.

Thinking of his remote cabin near a river and pond, Austin's water buffalo rumbled in his mind. It had been ages since he'd taken the time just to wallow in water. He could hardly wait.

He would have started his vacation earlier that week, but he hadn't wanted to miss Dane's wedding.

With that thought in mind, Austin hurried through the side door and into his attached garage. He stopped at the passenger door of his metallic-gold 1972 *T-top Stingray Corvette*. Adjusting the way he held the keys in his hand, he opened the door.

After placing his boots and bag on the floorboard, Austin closed the door and rounded the vehicle. He slid his fingertips along the hood of the classic car, smiling faintly. He looked forward to spending a couple of days racing along the curvy back roads.

Austin climbed behind the wheel, reached up, and pushed the button on the garage door opener attached to his sun visor. Hearing the door behind him rumble as it moved, he slid the key into the slot and brought his baby roaring to life. Austin ran his palms over the steering wheel for a few seconds, just enjoying being behind the wheel of his favorite toy.

It had taken him a couple of years to find just the right model he'd wanted and another four years to bring her back to her shining glory. The labor of love had been worth it, though. She looked amazing and ran like a gem.

His *Vette* was the one thing that could make him smile these days.

Hopefully, my vacation will help me put my loss behind me.

As Austin headed to Councilman Regales Colearian's estate where Dane and Danny's wedding would take place, he pondered just how the hell someone had managed to twist Gaston's beliefs around so badly. While Gaston had always been a bit on the bigoted side, Austin hadn't realized he'd become that indoctrinated. The pair of ex-councilmen who'd gone rogue had convinced a number of enforcers to go with them. They'd held the belief that Fate didn't pair those of the same sex. They'd also believed that shifters should have been at the top of the food chain. They were even willing to sell their own kind for experimentation to further their ends.

Fortunately, they're dead now, too.

He knew Ephram followed Gaston's lead like a puppy. The pair had always been that way. Gaston led, and Ephram followed.

If I'd known Gaston was going to follow the rogue councilmen, could I have stopped Ephram somehow?

With a dark sigh, Austin shook his head. While he probably couldn't have, he wished he'd at least noticed the changes in Gaston enough to have had a chance to try. Instead, Austin had allowed work and a few friends to take up most of his waking hours, hardly spending any time with his brothers, even while at Shifter Council headquarters.

Gripping the wheel tightly, Austin grumbled, "Too late. Can't change the past."

The gates to Regales's estate appeared to Austin's right, and he blinked in surprise. They were standing wide open. There were even balloons attached to the wrought iron fence on either side, the white and red objects waving in the wind.

"Huh. Okay." Austin turned his *Stingray* into the drive and rolled slowly forward. Spotting more balloons in the perfectly manicured trees, he smirked. "Guess they're going all out."

When Austin turned a bend in the driveway and approached the house, he finally spotted several men dressed in suits, recognizing all four of them as council enforcers. One stood on each side of a car stopped in the driveway, waiting for the people to exit. Then the man on the driver's side climbed behind the wheel and started forward, turning left onto the lawn where dozens of other vehicles were already parked.

Austin frowned, not pleased at the idea of someone else driving his baby.

Stopping where Enforcer Germaine indicated, the tall, slender anaconda shifter grinned broadly at him when Austin rolled down his window.

"Lucky me," Germaine quipped, eyeing his vehicle appreciatively. "I get to drive this beauty, even if it is only a few yards."

"Valet?" Austin grumbled, frowning upon seeing Germaine continue to grin at him. "Seriously? Can't I park myself?"

Germaine tipped his head back and laughed for a few seconds before turning his attention to another enforcer. "What do you think, Laudlin? Think he's okay to park himself?"

Laudlin—a beefy black bear shifter—tapped his forefinger on his chin. "I don't know. We're supposed to be inspecting the vehicles for bombs, you know."

"What?" Austin snapped. "Seriously? Bombs?"

Head Enforcer Mycroft rolled his eyes while shaking his head at their pairs' antics. "No way would Austin put a bomb in his baby." He waved his hand toward where Enforcer Rigel had parked the other car. "Go on. Rigel will point out where to park."

"Thank you." Austin tipped his head in deference to his boss, then started forward. As he rolled by Germaine, he flipped the man off, which only made the guy laugh again.

Seeing Rigel waiting at the corner of the car he'd just parked, the alligator shifter beckoning to him, Austin headed that way. After he'd parked where indicated, he rolled up his window and shut off his vehicle. Austin reached over and opened his duffel bag so he could pull out his card for the couple. There was a hundred-dollar gift card to a sporting goods store inside. With that in hand, he exited and locked his vehicle before shoving his keys into his pocket.

"What's with the valet parking?" Austin asked curiously, falling into step with Rigel.

Rigel flashed a smile his way, his white teeth gleaming in his deeply tanned face. "With the councilman's gates open for guests, we're making certain no unwelcome arrivals show up."

"Speaking of which." Mycroft checked the time on his phone. "Bought time we closed them. The ceremony should be starting in a few minutes."

Mycroft hit a few buttons on his phone, probably closing the gates electronically, just as another car came into view. Austin spotted another fellow enforcer behind the wheel — Lyra Kilopia, a tiger shifter — and Germaine moved to intercept her. She grinned and stopped her vehicle, happy to relinquish her car to Germaine.

"Well, damn," Austin muttered, unable to help the way his eyes widened. "Have you ever seen Lyra in a dress?"

"I have not," Rigel replied. "But it is a wedding."

"Right."

Austin couldn't take his eyes off Lyra — not because he was attracted to her, even though she was stunning, but because the sight was just too bizarre for words. At least, he thought so. As a kick-ass enforcer, she normally wore cargo pants with plenty of pockets — pockets full of weapons — and a black shirt that clung to her lithe torso.

Right then, instead of Lyra's normal ponytail, her dark-brown hair was swept in an artful up-do, held in place by a sparkly butterfly comb. She wore a blue and white floral sundress, which dipped to show off her cleavage. The flowing skirt barely reached her knees, showing off her long, toned legs, which were accented by a pair of white, high-heeled sandals. Even her toenails were painted white.

Laughing, Lyra touched Austin's jaw, causing him to snap it shut. "Well, I can see I've shocked the shit out of you all." Her blue eyes danced with mirth as she glanced around at everyone, and they were all nodding, Austin included. "Well, escort me, Austin. I don't have a date, either."

Snapping out of shock, Austin lifted his arm. "Known you over thirty years," he stated in his defense while Lyra placed her hand in the crook of his arm. "Never seen you like this. You look fantastic."

"Thank you," Lyra replied as they headed around the side of the estate house. "You clean up pretty nice yourself."

Austin chuckled low in his throat. "I'm still in jeans."

"But they're nice jeans," Lyra pointed out, glancing at him up and down. "They accentuate your fine ass."

Curving his lips into a smirk, Austin murmured, "Thanks." He indicated the wrapped box she carried in her other hand. "What'd you get them?"

"This is a tranq dart gun for Danny."

Austin grinned broadly as he nodded. "Nice."

With a number of enforcers finding human mates, tranq dart guns for protection were becoming popular. After all, not all shifters were too pleased by the acceptance of same-sex pairings or even mating with humans in general. Some things were just slow to change.

When they rounded the side of the house, Austin saw rows of seating set up, and most of the chairs were already full. Councilman Regales stood beside the flower-laden arch at the end of the aisle, and Enforcer Dane stood beside him. Both were in suits—Regales in black while Dane's was white.

"Damn," Lyra murmured. "We're later than I thought. Come on."

Austin hurried forward with her, silently agreeing. They found seats at the back and settled into place just in time to have to stand again for Danny's appearance. Austin still didn't understand the fascination with getting married, but he had to admit, Danny's smile appeared radiant as he stared at Dane and made his way down the aisle.

Just as Austin retook his seat, a gentle breeze kicked up. He scented the flowers decorating the arch as well as the unique smells of the different breeds of shifters around him. There were several vampires, too.

And something else.

Underneath all that, Austin found his attention captured by a pleasant aroma of pine mixed with . . . grease. Inhaling deeply, he took in more of that scent. His gut tightened, and his blood heated. As Austin breathed in the smell a third time, his water buffalo rumbled in the back of his mind, urging him to find the source of the smell.

It hit him like a brick upside the head.

Holy shit. My mate is here somewhere.

As much as Austin wanted to do exactly as his animal urged, he knew he couldn't. The ceremony had started. As Dane shared how he was the luckiest shifter in existence, Austin discreetly swept his gaze over the crowd.

There were only a few people in the seats that he didn't recognize. His attention bounced between a slender female in the second row to the right, and a tawny-colored-haired man sitting with a group that he knew lived at Councilman Vincentius Goldstein's estate. He found his focus riveting on that man, and his water buffalo rumbled his appreciation.

Anticipation flooded him at the chance to meet the guy.

Looks like I'm staying for the reception after all.

CHAPTER TWO

Listening to Dane and Danny exchange vows, Pete Saugner lifted the tissue to his right eye and dabbed carefully. He did his best not to sniffle as a mixture of happiness and jealousy swirled through him, making him emotional. Ruthlessly pushing away the latter, Pete focused on the former.

I'm so very happy for them.

He'd met Dane on several occasions when the large Komodo dragon shifter had come to Councilman Vincentius's home. He'd even worked on the man's motorcycle. His black *Harley Electra Road Glide* was a thing of beauty.

Pete had been happy for Dane when he'd found his mate in Danny. Everyone deserved to find that special someone.

Wish I could find mine.

Upon thinking that, Pete felt a wash of guilt. He had a good life. A lot better than it had been a couple of years prior. Learning about shifters and the paranormal had opened his world in a way he never would have dreamed.

Just because Pete hadn't found his mate in any of the guys he'd met, that was okay. He had a make-shift family with the others who lived at Vincentius's estate with them. Not to mention free room and board, free food, and a great wage.

And I get to work on some sweet rides.

Pete loved being a mechanic. In high school, he'd discovered an affinity for all things mechanical. From small engines to huge machines, they just seemed to speak to him.

When Councilman Regales pronounced the couple as Dane and Danny Drudeson, Pete grinned broadly and clapped right along with everyone else. Dane wrapped his arm around Danny's waist and pulled him in for another kiss, and a number of wolf whistles rent the air. Then the pair headed down the aisle, both of them grinning like loons.

Maybe someday I'll have something like that.

In truth, Pete would be happy with a fuck buddy so he didn't have to keep using his right hand. Unfortunately, he wasn't too keen on bars or nightclubs. The guys had taken him a few times, but he had two left feet and didn't feel comfortable with the idea of a bathroom hook-up.

"Come on," Ashton encouraged, touching Pete's upper arm. "Let's head over and grab some food and a table. They're going to be a while taking pictures."

Pete nodded and followed Cho to the left and out of their row, who was holding hands with his mate, Vincentius. The pair seemed like an unlikely couple — until you realized they both loved computers. They could sit in their computer room together for hours without coming out.

Wonder how much sex those computers have monitored.

Mentally rolling his eyes at his silly thought, Pete glanced around at all the happy, smiling people. He knew most of them were shifters. There were a few vampires and humans thrown in, too. Pete figured most of them worked for the Shifter Council in one capacity or another, just like him.

Pete went with the flow and ended up at the buffet. He chatted with those on his left and right, sharing comments about how happy he was for the couple as well as how lovely the ceremony was. Picking up a plastic plate, he moved along with everyone, choosing a couple of turkey sandwich triangles, along with a couple of sides. He avoided the pasta salad, since he didn't like tuna fish.

At the end of the line, there were a number of drink options, and Pete snagged a red fruit punch flavored drink.

Stepping out of the line, Pete headed for the table after the other guys.

"Hey, Pete," a deep voice called. "Got a minute?"

Pete turned and spotted Germaine next to him. "Hey, Germaine." He had to tip his head way back to meet the tall, black man's gaze. "What's up?"

Germaine rubbed the back of his neck and grimaced. "Now probably isn't the best time, but I figured since we're both here, I'd just ask."

Concern filled Pete upon spotting the normally confident man's clear discomfort. "Whatever it is, I'm sure it's fine," he stated, trying to set the other guy's mind at ease. "Hit me with it."

Nodding, Germaine told him, "I've noticed an odd pulling to the left on one of the council SUVs. Do you know if you have time in your schedule to take a look at it soon?"

"Oh. I should." Pete tipped his head to the side and mentally cataloged his workload. With a smile at the guy, he told him, "If you bring it in Tuesday afternoon, I can take a look first thing Wednesday."

Germaine grinned, appearing relieved. "Thanks, man. I appreciate it."

"You're welcome," Pete replied, smiling back at him. "Happy to help."

After patting Pete on the upper arm, Germaine turned and headed away. Pete watched him a moment, seeing the way he paused to wrap his arm around his shifter mate—Sage. Germaine even paused to peck a kiss to Sage's lips.

Pete turned away, fighting back a sigh. There were so many happy couples around him. At times, it was so very difficult not to feel jealous.

Reaching the table, Pete found a seat and placed his food and drink before him. He took a bite of the potato salad and enjoyed the rich flavor. Allowing the conversation to flow around him, Pete focused on his food as he peered around at the other guests.

Pete found his attention snagged by someone Germaine was talking to. The guy appeared to be only an inch shorter than the snake shifter, making him around six-foot-five. He was far broader, though, with thick, medium-brown hair hanging in waves around his face. His goatee and massive frame gave him a dangerous air.

He's totally gotta be an enforcer.

A fissure of arousal surged through Pete's veins. He'd always had a thing for big men. Too bad he was afraid of them. After getting beaten up one too many times in the high school locker room, he avoided macho-looking strangers.

When the man in question peered in Pete's direction, he quickly lowered his gaze to his plate and speared another bite of potato salad.

"Someone got your attention?" Ashton's mate, Ranger, asked, teasing in his tone. He even nudged Pete's arm.

"Uh, no," Pete replied. "Just people watching in general."

Ranger gave him a look that totally told Pete he was about to call him on his bullshit answer.

Right. Shifters can smell deceit. Crap.

"Don't give me that." Ranger tapped the side of his nose. "For a sec there, you were attracted to someone."

Scowling at Ranger, Pete grumbled, "You're not supposed to comment on stuff like that."

Smirking, Ranger replied, "If I don't comment on it, how am I supposed to help you talk to the guy?"

"I'm sure he's not interested in a twink like me," Pete countered.

"You don't know that," Ranger replied, his lips curving into a frown. "Are you putting yourself down? Because that's not cool. You're a cute guy."

"Cute." Pete sighed and shook his head. "The death knell to any guy."

Ranger cocked his head. "Huh?"

Scoffing, Pete explained, "Puppies and kittens are supposed to be cute. Not guys."

"Some guys like cute."

Snapping his attention to the left, Pete had to look up . . . way up. A jolt of fear flashed through him when he met the dark-eyed gaze of the huge stranger. Looking across the yard at him, Pete thought he was hot. With him looming over him, not so much.

The goateed man's nostrils flared, and his brows shot up. He even took a step backward. When he lifted his hands, palms out, Pete flinched.

"Shit, baby," the guy rumbled. "I'm not gonna hurt you. You're my mate." He hesitated a second before asking, "Can't you smell our connection?"

We're mates? Really?

"Pete is human," Ranger answered after a few heartbeats, when it became obvious that Pete couldn't find his tongue. The jackal shifter held out his hand. "I'm Ranger. And you are?"

"I'm Austin O'Malley," the huge man replied, taking Ranger's hand. Then he held it out to Pete. "And I hear you're Pete Saugner. Best damn mechanic around these parts."

Forcing himself to move, Pete hesitantly reached out and took Austin's hand. "I-I don't know about that," he murmured, surprised to feel warm tingles traveling up his arm. Even the hairs on his forearm stood on end.

"Well, that's what Germaine claimed," Austin replied. Continuing to hold Pete's hand, he brushed his thumb back and forth on his skin. "It's a pleasure to meet you, Pete."

"Y-You, too," Pete whispered back.

"Austin." Vincentius clapped Austin on the shoulder, announcing his arrival to the table. "I see you're being introduced to Pete. Don't tell me there's something wrong with that pretty *Stingray* of yours."

Austin shook his head. "Nope." A smile curved up the

sides of his goateed lips, and he still didn't release Pete. "Scented Pete from across the way. He's my mate."

Vincentius's eyes widened, and his brows lifted. "You don't say." He then glanced where they still clasped hands to Pete's face. "You're looking a little shell-shocked there, Pete. You okay, son?"

Pete cleared his throat and tugged lightly, trying to free his hand. It took a second, third tug for Austin to release him. "Yes, sir," he replied, pleased his voice didn't squeak. "Just, uh. Yep. Shocked." Squinting up at Austin, Pete couldn't help but comment, "Um, I know that mates are picked by Fate and all, so you don't really have much of a say. Are you, uh, are you okay to be paired with someone like me?"

"Someone like you?" Austin's thick eyebrows furrowed. "What are you talking about? A mechanic?"

"No." Pete shook his head. "I mean, look at you." He waved a hand in Austin's general direction before indicating himself to emphasize his point. "And look at me."

Austin shook his head once more. "I'm sorry, Pete. I'm not following." Before Pete could try again, Austin added, "You know about shifters and mates, right? You already stated that they're picked by Fate."

"Well, yeah."

Pete was having a hard time thinking clearly with the huge man so close to him—and it wasn't all caused by the fear he continued to experience. A slow burn of arousal was beginning to warm his gut. He liked how Austin continued to focus on him, his dark eyes warm and intense.

Lifting his huge hand, Austin pointed at the guys around the table. "And your friends are mated, so you don't have a problem with them being gay." Then his brows furrowed even further. "Is that the problem? You're not gay?"

Barking a laugh, Pete quickly shook his head. "Oh, I'm

gay," he assured, continuing to chuckle. "So very gay." Sobering, Pete finally blurted out, "But you're big and brawny and sexy, and I'm . . . well, a twink. How could you be happy with that?"

Austin's full lips parted in a wide grin. "Oh, Pete. I love the fact that you'll fit in my arms." Easing a step closer, he lifted a hand toward him. When Pete couldn't stop from tensing, Austin grimaced as he paused and rumbled, "And someone hurt you, my mate."

Pete nodded, eyeing Austin's hand. While he would love to feel the big man's touch, he feared it, too. Shifters had enhanced strength and speed.

What if he isn't gentle? He could hurt me so bad, even if by accident.

Sighing, Austin slowly lowered his hand to his side, a pained expression creasing his features.

"Why don't you join us, Austin," Vincentius urged, guiding Cho into a chair. He pointed at the one to the right of Pete, where the guys were shifting down a chair to make room. "That way, Pete can get to know you."

Austin glanced at the councilman as he nodded slowly before refocusing on Pete. "Is that okay with you, Pete?"

Pete nodded. "Yeah. Thanks."

What looked suspiciously like relief filled Austin's features. He crossed behind Pete, then took the vacated chair. When Austin appeared to sit carefully, the thing creaked under his weight.

The man wasn't fat. He was just . . . *big*.

Austin's smile appeared a bit rueful. "These things aren't built for a man of my proportions."

That seemed to break the ice, and everyone around the table chuckled.

Pete felt himself relaxing.

"Can I get you something to eat or drink, Austin?" Ashton asked from Ranger's other side.

Opening his mouth, Austin hesitated, seeming to give that some thought. "Uh, how about just a beer," he told the other shifter. "I'm not hungry at the moment."

"Not hungry?" Hess teased, smirking at Austin. The Kodiak bear shifter's own plate was piled high with food. "Ain't that part of the reason we enjoy a wedding reception? Food you don't normally make yourself?"

Austin chuckled, dipping his head in a quick nod. "Usually. But I wasn't planning on staying for the reception."

"Why not?" Gilbert, Hess's mate, asked bluntly.

Resting his forearms on the table, Austin folded his hands. "My vacation starts today. I was planning on staying for the wedding, offering my congrats, then heading into the mountains to spend some time in animal form." Austin smiled as he peered at Pete. "But it looks like my plans have changed."

"Because you scented me?" Pete guessed quietly.

Austin dipped his head in a nod. "Exactly right."

Pete cocked his head. "You'd change your vacation plans just because you met me?"

Nodding again, Austin smiled at him. "You're a gift from the gods, Pete." He glanced around at the other couples before refocusing on him. "Have you been around when any of the other couples found their mates?"

Glancing at the others, seeing most of them smiling encouragingly, Pete admitted, "A few of them."

Pete recalled how when the human Reese had met Seever—a lion shifter employed by Vincentius—the man hadn't even returned to his hometown to serve out a two-week notice on his job. The man was now the councilman's chef. In fact, if Pete recalled correctly, he hadn't even gone back to Colin City in Colorado to pack his own home. Several members of the guys' flock, along with his cousin Rocky, had gone instead.

"I—"

Before Pete could finish his thought, although he wasn't entirely certain what he would say, his phone vibrated in his pocket. Recalling he'd turned off the ring for the wedding ceremony, he pulled it out and looked at the screen. Surprise mixed with dread flooded his gut as he looked at who the text had been from.

Detective Oliver Morrison.

With a tremble in his hands, Pete opened the text. His breathing sped up as he read the man's message.

Call me when you have a few minutes. I just received word that Winston is out of jail on parole.

"Hey, what is it?" Austin crooned, resting his hand on Pete's back and lightly rubbing up and down his spine. "What's happened?"

To Pete's surprise, he found the man's touch soothing. He even managed to find his tongue.

As Pete peered around the table, seeing everyone's concerned looks, he murmured, "That was Detective Morrison. Winston is out on parole."

The table erupted in shouts of denial and cursing.

CHAPTER THREE

Austin swept his gaze over the clearly upset occupants of the table. While he didn't know who that was or why it was important, he did appreciate that it allowed him to finally touch his mate. He figured Pete didn't even realize it, but his skittish human was even pressing into his palm, taking support and comfort from his touch.

Finally, Vincentius held up his hand, and the table fell silent. "Is that all the detective told you?"

Pete swallowed so hard that his Adam's apple bobbed. The move drew Austin's attention to it, and his mouth watered. He wanted to suck on that nub in the worst way, but he knew Pete wasn't anywhere near ready for that, yet.

Plus, from the acrid scent of fear pouring off of Pete damn near in waves, Austin knew he needed to settle his mate before anything could happen.

This must be why Fate gave me my mate now. He needs me.

"That's all," Pete murmured. After clearing his throat, he added, "He asked me to call him when I have a minute."

Unable to hold his tongue—after all, Austin needed information to soothe his mate—he asked, "Who's Winston?"

Growling softly, Hess curled his lip. "An asshole."

Vincentius's eyes narrowed, expressing his distaste without words. "Let's just say . . . they attacked Pete."

They?

"It's okay," Pete whispered. He even leaned toward Austin, looking at him side-eyed. "Is your touch soothing because of the mate thing?"

Austin nodded. "It is." Offering his human a reassuring smile, he told him, "And I appreciate that it does, and I can be here for you in your time of need."

Pete nibbled his bottom lip for a few seconds before tipping his head in a single nod. "Winston and his friend, Leeson, they tried to rape me. Thad and Lachlan stopped them. That's how I met everyone."

His voice was pitched so low that Austin could barely hear the man. When he did decipher Pete's words, he gritted his teeth to hold back his growl. His water buffalo bellowed angrily in the back of his mind, and he agreed with his animal. If he ever came across this Winston character — or his friend — he would extract restitution shifter style.

"I thought he was supposed to be in for at least twelve years before he had a chance at parole. Him and Leeson both," Cho commented, his eyes wide with concern. "That's what the courts decreed. How can Winston be out after only a few years?"

Blowing out a breath, Vincentius grumbled, "Guess my decision to have their memories altered and turn them over to the human police was a mistake." He frowned as he eyed Pete. "I'm sorry, Pete."

"It's not your fault," Pete whispered before turning his attention to Austin. "Guess you're sorry to have met me now."

"What do you mean?" Austin wasn't following.

With a shrug, Pete wrapped his arms around his waist. "Just mean the drama this may cause." He grimaced. "I hope he won't come after me again, but . . ." His words trailed off as his voice grew quieter.

"If he comes after you, I'll deal with him," Austin assured, unable to help the slight growl that entered his voice. He continued to run his palm over Pete's back. "You're my mate, and I will take care of you."

Pete's smile appeared tremulous even as he stated, "I can't

expect you to do that."

Scoffing, Ashton leaned forward and eyed Pete. "Pete, you surely *can* expect Austin to do that. He's your mate." The American kestrel shifter pinned him with a kind smile. "You're a gift from Fate, remember? His natural instinct is to care for you, to keep you safe" — then Ashton waggled his eyebrows — "and, of course, to give you pleasure."

As Austin watched, he saw pink infuse Pete's cheeks. He also noticed how the sweet scent of arousal began to beat out the fear. His own libido surged in response, making him shift in his seat as his cock thickened behind the fly of his jeans.

"Hey, it looks like the pictures are done," Ranger pointed out. "Dane and Danny are sitting and eating now."

Austin followed Ranger's line of sight and saw Dane and Danny cuddled close. His brothers, Dakota and Delanrue, were there as well as Delanrue's small guinea pig shifter mate, Miggs. The group laughed and talked, grinning and teasing.

Damn. Delanrue actually knows how to laugh.

He'd never seen that before. The shifter interrogator was known as the stoic one, cold and unapproachable. Every time he peered at Miggs however, the chill in his hazel eyes warmed. The love in Miggs's eyes when he returned Delanrue's regard was just as plain to see.

Turning his attention back to Pete, Austin hoped that he and Pete would be like that soon. Instead, he still saw the haunted look in his pretty human's brown eyes. His fingers twitched with the desire to pull the small man onto his lap, cradling him close and promising no one would ever harm him again.

Would he let me?

Austin knew Pete would fit perfectly against him. Watching him talk with Germaine, he guessed that Pete couldn't be more than five-foot-four. The form-fitting jeans and cut of his button-down shirt revealed a slender frame. Pete truly was the epitome of a twink, and Austin could hardly wait to explore every inch of his body.

"I suppose I should give them my regards and leave," Pete murmured, frowning. "I sure don't feel like dancing anymore." Scoffing, he muttered, "Even if I could dance."

"Don't like to dance?" Austin asked curiously, eager to learn anything he could about his mate.

"Um, not that I don't *like* to," Pete replied with a grimace. Meeting his gaze, he admitted, "I have two left feet."

Smiling down at Pete, Austin told him, "We could just stand and sway." With an eyebrow waggle, he stated, "I'm great at swaying."

To Austin's pleasure, Pete snickered. "Sway, huh?"

With a shrug, Austin nodded. "Sure. Besides, now that I'm here, that cake looks awfully good."

"Got a sweet tooth, Austin?"

"I do," Austin admitted. Fighting his own blush, he continued, "Love cinnamon bears, gum drops, Swedish fish. All those things."

"Me, too," Pete replied softly. "I always buy some sort of gummy when I go to the movies."

"Oh, yeah?" Austin picked up the beer someone had put on the table before him a little while ago. He used the excuse to lean closer to Pete. "When was the last time you went to the movies? What was it?"

"Ummm." Pete seemed to be thinking hard before naming the title of an action flick. "That was back when I was in vocational school for being a mechanic with a few guys who I thought were my friends."

"Thought?" Austin narrowed his eyes. There was a story there. "Why thought?"

Scoffing, Pete answered. "Because after I finished vocational school to become a mechanic, I came out officially." With a roll of his eyes, he claimed, "Guess thinking there's a possibility your son is gay is totally different than having it confirmed. I was disowned, and all those *friends"* — Pete made air quotes — "disappeared real fast."

"Damn," Austin grumbled. "Sorry to hear that."

With a shrug, Pete admitted, "It's how I ended up in Savannah. I got hired on at a mechanic shop here. Found an apartment and worked hard." He frowned as he muttered, "Too bad I couldn't pick my neighbors."

"Neighbors?" Austin jumped on that. Even as he felt damn grateful Pete had ended up in Savannah, he wanted to find his mate's parents and smack some sense into them.

"Winston and Leeson rented a two-bedroom down the hall from my one-bedroom."

As soon as Austin growled softly, Pete stiffened.

"Relax, my mate," Austin purred, resuming his rubbing on Pete's back. He even took a chance, dipped his head, and pressed a kiss to his neck. "I know I'm a big man," he murmured into Pete's ear. "But you are my mate. I would never hurt you. You'll always be safe with me."

"What about by accident?" Pete countered, turning his head just a little so he could stare at him out of the corner of his eyes. "You're a paranormal with increased strength. I'm just a small human."

"You are not *just* anything, Pete," Austin countered, disliking the way his mate dismissed himself that way. "You are a gifted mechanic and a friend to many." Pecking another kiss to his neck, Austin added, "And you're my mate, and I'm so very grateful to have finally met you."

As a Council Enforcer, Austin was normally assigned to tasks for Councilmen Regales and Lorian. He didn't usually interact with Councilman Vincentius. That would explain why he hadn't been at Vincentius's home at the same time as Pete had been about.

"You're just saying that because Fate deemed me your

mate," Pete whispered.

Although Austin enjoyed the way Pete tipped his head to the side to offer more room, he didn't like his mate's dismissiveness of his words.

Someone's done a number on my mate's confidence.

Austin glanced at the others around the table, pleased to see that they didn't appear too thrilled with Pete's words, either.

"I think I'd really like to go," Pete muttered, his voice turning husky. "I need to call the detective and see what's going on."

"I'll drive you," Austin immediately offered. "Germaine said you live at Vincentius's estate." He glanced toward the councilman and spotted the lion shifter dipping his chin in a small nod. Returning his focus to Pete, Austin added, "I'd love to cuddle up with you while you make your call. Offer support."

"Um, thanks?" Pete didn't sound so sure, but at least he wasn't flinching from him anymore.

"We'll join you," Ashton stated, rising from his seat, Ranger doing the same.

Vincentius rose as well. "I'll come, too." He threaded his fingers through Cho's hair and smiled adoringly at his guinea fowl shifter mate. "Would you like to stay with Hector and Rocky to do some dancing, my mate?"

Cho stuck out his bottom lip. "It won't be the same without you."

"I know, my sweet," Vincentius murmured. "And I'm sorry." Bending at the waist, he pecked a kiss to his mate's lips. "But we must take care of our friend's needs."

Instantly, Cho's disappointment cleared. "I understand. We can dance at home." His expression turned heated as he gained his feet. "While naked."

Vincentius hummed as he slid his arm around Cho's waist. "I do like the way you think."

Cho giggled.

Austin rose when Pete did. Unfortunately, the reminder of his size seemed to hit his mate, for he shrank back from him.

Taking Pete's hand in his own, Austin threaded their fingers. "You asked if I'd ever accidentally hurt you." He recalled he hadn't really answered his mate's question. Lightly squeezing Pete's hand, Austin assured, "Absolutely not. Now that I've met you, you're everything to me." Seeing Pete's disbelieving expression, he added, "That means I'll always be on the lookout to take care of your needs, and your safety is at the top of that list."

Pete held his gaze for a long moment, his gaze roving over his face. He was obviously searching for something.

Austin patiently held the other man's attention, waiting, hoping he accepted the truth between them.

Finally, Pete offered him a tremulous smile. "Okay."

Unable to help himself, Austin grinned broadly. "Okay." Lifting Pete's hand to his lips, he pressed a kiss to it. "Let's go offer the grooms our congratulations."

After nodding, Pete turned to his friends still seated at the table. "I'll see you guys at the house later."

They nodded, assuring Pete they'd catch up with him as soon as they arrived home.

As Austin and the others moved away from the table, Hess called, "Hey, Austin."

Pausing, Austin peered over his shoulder at the bear shifter, seeing the serious gleam in his eyes. "You take good care of our friend, man."

Austin smiled and dipped his chin in a nod. "Of that, you can be assured," he promised.

Hess then gave him a lecherous smile and a wink.

Rolling his eyes, Austin began moving again, ever-so-pleased to still have Pete's hand in his own.

One way or another, Austin hoped Pete would soon grow

used to his touch.

Austin, Pete, and the others made their way to the head table. They had to wait a few minutes, since the grooms were chatting with some others. As they waited, Austin continued to rub his thumb over the back of Pete's hand soothingly.

"Well, well, Austin," Dane called, drawing his attention. "When did you meet Pete?" He waggled his brows playfully as he continued, "And why are you holding his hand?"

Smiling a smidge, Austin replied smugly, "I just met Pete today, and I'm holding his hand because he's my mate." He cast a grin at Pete as he added, "We're going to head to his place so we can talk and get to know each other."

Austin had every intention of following through on his words, so it wasn't a lie.

"Well, damn, man," Dakota burst out, his brows sky-rocketing nearly to his forehead. "Congrats, you son-of-a-bitch." Just as fast, he grinned broadly. "I'm damn jealous, but Pete's a great man." Dakota winked as he added, "Plus, if anything happens to your *Vette*, he'll be able to fix it."

"Oh, what kind of *Corvette* do you have?" Pete asked curiously.

"A seventy-two T-top *Stingray*," Austin replied proudly, liking the sound of Pete's impressed whistle. While Austin had never let anyone else work on his baby, for his mate, he would make an exception. "She's a beaut."

"I bet," Pete murmured. Then he focused on Dane again. "Congrats on your wedding. The ceremony was wonderful." With a soft laugh, Pete told them, "Your vows made me tear up. Beautiful."

"Thanks for coming, Pete," Danny replied. "And thank you." He focused on Dane, his smile full of love. "And I had to blink back a few tears, too."

"Anything for you, baby," Dane rumbled before pressing a chaste kiss to Danny's lips. Then he grinned at them again.

"So glad you were able to connect." He sobered, focusing on Austin. "You deserve something good in your life, man. Congratulations."

A pang of pain twisted in his chest as he dipped his chin in a curt nod. While he noticed the question in Pete's eyes, he didn't comment on it. Austin would share everything eventually, but now wasn't the time.

They talked for a few more minutes, as did Vincentius, Cho, Ashton, and Ranger. Then they said their goodbyes. After all, there were others waiting to congratulate the newlyweds.

Still holding Pete's hand, Austin guided his mate away from the party.

CHAPTER FOUR

Pete didn't know if leaving with Austin was the best idea. He probably should have ridden with his friends. Except, when he'd seen the vintage, gold T-top *Corvette* parked amidst all the cars, he'd been drawn to it like a magnet.

As a mechanic, Pete loved cars. Old ones were the best, although he managed to fix new ones just fine. To him, older vehicles just seemed purer, without the hassle of computers with all sorts of extra electrical gadgets that could cause problems.

That was why, when Austin guided Pete to the vehicle's passenger side and opened the door, he didn't think twice about sliding in. It was a little cramped due to the duffle bag and boots on the floor, but he didn't mind. He was a small guy, after all.

To Pete's surprise, Austin leaned in and buckled his seatbelt for him, then finished by pecking a kiss to his temple.

Pete stared at Austin as he rounded the hood of the vehicle. He seemed so sincere in all his actions. At times, his voice had sounded laced with awe as they'd talked at the table.

Can I trust him?

With the way the big man turned him on, Pete sure hoped so. Plus, his friends seemed to be taking Austin at his word. The man—shifter—claimed they were mates. He knew how important that was to paranormals. They didn't joke about it, and if Austin had been lying, his friends would have called him out on it immediately.

So, I have a mate of my own.

Once Austin had settled behind the wheel and brought the classic car to life—flashing a smile Pete's way a couple of times—he started them out of the driveway. He followed behind Vincentius's SUV without a word. The rumble of the *Vette*'s engine relaxed Pete, and he found himself admiring the vehicle's interior.

"How long have you had it?" Pete asked, unable to contain his curiosity.

Austin obviously knew to what Pete was referring, for he answered, "Eight years. She was pretty rundown at the time. Didn't always start, the interior was trashed from rodents, and her paint was faded from too much time in the sun." Wincing at what must have been his memories, Austin continued, "It took me years to get her looking and sounding like she does. Did everything myself."

Pete watched as Austin ran his hand over the dash. The smile on his face told him how much the man appreciated his vehicle. He could only imagine the blood and sweat that had gone into it.

"A labor of love," Pete mused softly.

Flashing a grin Pete's way, Austin nodded. "Exactly."

"So, what kind of shifter are you?" Pete asked, cocking his head. "Something big."

"Oh." Austin grinned broadly at him. "A water buffalo."

Nodding slowly, Pete racked his brain. "Uh, I'm not totally sure I know what that looks like," he admitted. "It's not a bison, right?"

"No, definitely different than an American bison," Austin replied, a smile twitching the sides of his goateed lips. "Let's see, uh, a large cattle-type animal with sweeping horns." He shrugged, telling him, "A little hard to describe unless you see it, I guess. You could google for water buffalo pictures, or I can shift for you at the councilman's estate."

"You'd shift for me?" Pete rolled his eyes and waved a

hand dismissively. "That was a silly question." Scoffing, he quickly added, "The guys love to shift and play in animal form."

Austin nodded. "We do enjoy spending time in our animal form." Glancing Pete's way, he added, "And my bull would very much like to meet you at some point."

"Are water buffalo wild?" Pete shifted in his seat so he partially faced Austin, folding his hands in his lap. "Or domesticated?"

"Both," Austin replied. As he continued talking, he slowly reached over and rested his big hand over both of Pete's, the hold warm and powerful. "There are wild herds in India and Southeast Asia, but water buffalo have been domesticated for centuries in the tropics to pull carts, ride, and pack."

"Wow. Versatile."

Pete murmured the words, his attention drifting to where Austin held him. Taking a chance, he untwined his own fingers so he could turn one hand over. Clasping Austin's much larger hand in his own, he squeezed lightly.

Ever-so-gently, Austin squeezed back.

"So," Pete mused quietly. "I'm your mate."

Austin nodded once. "You're my mate." With a wink, he added, "That means I'm your mate, too."

Nodding, Pete felt heat unfurl in his stomach. He took in a deep breath before letting it out slowly. Then he stared at Austin, really taking him in.

The big, broad-shouldered man dominated the reasonably small cab of the *Corvette*. His head nearly brushed the glass T-top. His dark-brown hair hung in waves around his face, thick and shiny.

Pete dug the fingers of his free hand into his thigh, fighting his urge to run his fingers through it. He wondered if Austin would let him. Then he realized the man probably would, since it would make Pete happy, and shifters were all about making their mates happy.

"Um, do shifters try to make their mate happy to the detriment of themselves?"

Frowning, Austin glanced toward Pete before returning his attention to the road. "I'm not entirely certain I understand your question, Pete." When Pete nibbled his lip uncertainly, Austin squeezed his hand and asked, "Can you try another variation of that question?"

Blowing out a breath, Pete tried again. "I mean, I was just thinking about your hair."

"My hair?" Now Austin sounded confused. "What about it?"

"Well, it's stunning, and I want to touch it," Pete admitted. Feeling his cheeks heat, knowing he blushed, he hurried to finish. "I wanted to run my fingers through it, and I wondered if you'd let me. Then I realized you would because you're a shifter, and you'd want to please me." Cocking his head, Pete quickly finished, "But what if you don't like people playing with your hair? Would you let me do it because I'm your mate, even though you didn't like it?"

"Ahhh," Austin rumbled. Warmth was filling his dark eyes as he stopped at a red light and focused on Pete. "I love the idea of you threading your fingers through my hair. You touching me anywhere would please me." He winked, then added, "But I don't think that's actually what you were asking. So the simple answer is yes and no."

Pete frowned. "That's not an answer."

Austin sighed as he refocused on the road and the green light, moving them forward. "What I mean is, if you wanted to do something that I didn't like"—he squinted, perhaps thinking hard—"for example, riding a roller coaster. I don't like them."

"Wow, really?" Pete couldn't help his surprise. "Why?"

"I'm a big guy, Pete." Austin pointed out the obvious. "I'm

six-foot-five and two-hundred-eighty pounds of muscle. The seats are not built for a man of my proportions, so they're uncomfortable." Before Pete could do more than mumble a soft *wow* upon hearing Austin's dimensions, the other man added, "And I also don't care for the *lose your stomach* feeling you get when going down those big hills."

"Huh." Pete had always thought that was cool. Trying to follow along, he admitted, "And I like roller coasters, not that I've been on one in years." He'd needed every penny to make rent and put food on the table. "So if I wanted to ride one?"

"If you wanted to ride a roller coaster, I would find someone I trusted to go with you," Austin told him with a smile. "Then I'd wait at the bottom for you and kiss you when you got done."

Pete gaped at Austin. "You would?"

"Yes." Austin squeezed Pete's hand gently. "I don't want to control you or stop you from doing things you enjoy. I just want you safe while doing it."

Shaking his head, Pete told him, "That's not what I meant."

Austin's brows furrowed as he glanced at him. "Then what?"

"Would you really kiss me?"

"Of course," Austin replied immediately. "You're my mate. I hope to kiss you often." His goateed lips curved into a slight frown. "Do you not enjoy kissing?"

While Pete knew that some men felt that way, he wasn't one of them. "I enjoy kissing." He personally thought a good kiss could be more personal than sex. "I just meant, you'd kiss me in public?"

Austin immediately nodded. "If you'd allow it."

"Yeah, yeah," Pete hurried to say. "Of course, I'd allow it."

"Good."

That seemed to settle it, and right on time. They were pull-

31

ing up to Vincentius's estate, the gate opening for the councilman's SUV. Austin followed closely. While Vincentius parked in one of the garage bays, Austin began parking off to the side.

Suddenly, a second bay door opened, revealing an open bay and a waving Ashton. Evidently, the man had hurried from the SUV to open it for Austin.

"That's nice of him," Austin murmured. Glancing at the sky, he grimaced. "Especially since it looks like a storm is blowing in."

"Bummer," Pete commented. "I hope Dane and Danny's reception doesn't get rained out."

Austin shook his head. "There's plenty of room inside Regales's estate. They'll just move indoors."

Pete nodded. That made sense.

Once Austin parked and shut off the *Corvette*, Pete pushed from the vehicle. He gently closed the door before taking a moment to slide his hand over the swooping hood panel.

It really was a stunning piece of machinery.

Austin appeared at his side and took his free hand. "Come on," he urged, his expression turning serious. "We have a phone call to make."

Just that fast, the peace Pete had found while on the drive home disappeared. His pulse sped up, and a lump formed in his throat. He swallowed convulsively, trying to clear it, as he nodded and allowed Austin to guide him into the house, following the others.

Vincentius led the way into a comfortably appointed living area and immediately crossed to the sideboard. "Anyone want anything?" He began pulling out tumblers and stemware.

"We'll just grab a couple of beers," Ashton replied, indicating himself and Ranger. Crossing to the small fridge under the counter, he retrieved them himself.

"I'll take a beer," Austin stated, and Ashton pulled one for him, too.

"Wine, please. Red," Pete requested, although he hoped he didn't really need the liquid courage for the upcoming conversation.

Nodding, Vincentius opened a bottle and poured it into two glasses. He handed one to Cho before picking up his tumbler of bourbon and the other glass. Holding the wine out to Pete, he took it gratefully.

After taking a tentative sip, Pete took a larger one. He rolled the smooth liquid over his tongue, enjoying the robust flavor. There was just a hint of a bite at the end, and he hummed appreciatively.

"A malbec?" Pete guessed.

Vincentius nodded and smiled. "You're getting pretty good at that."

Pete scoffed, shaking his head. "I'm getting good at knowing which are Cho's favorites. Thad prefers cabernet."

Chuckling, Vincentius nodded. "Okay. Let's get settled, and we'll get this over with." Then he headed to a love seat and relaxed with Cho beside him.

Ashton and Ranger took another love seat, leaving a couple of large sofas as well as a pair of cushioned recliners. To Pete's confusion, he felt Austin pull him toward one of the chairs. After he'd placed his beer bottle on the end table, he took Pete's wine and did the same. Finally, Austin relaxed into the chair.

When he gripped Pete's waist and lifted him onto his lap, Pete would forever deny his squeak of surprise.

Austin wrapped his brawny arms around Pete's waist, tucking him close. "I like this," he rumbled into his ear while nuzzling his goatee against Pete's temple. "This okay?"

Was it?

Pete had seen several couples cuddle like this on many occasions. Rocky loved holding Hector on his lap. Occasionally, so did Vincentius and Cho.

After a second of hesitation, Pete nodded. "Yeah," he whispered. "This is okay."

With their size differences, sitting on Austin's thick thighs was even reasonably comfortable. What was really nice was the gentle way Austin petted Pete's side and nuzzled him. His warmth cocooned him, helping Pete to relax.

"Pete?" Vincentius began. "Why don't you put the call on speaker?"

Nodding, Pete pulled out his phone. As soon as he woke the device, Detective Morrison's last message filled the screen. After taking a deep breath, which allowed him to enjoy Austin's rich, masculine scent, Pete hit the call button.

The phone rang once, twice, three times.

For an instant, Pete feared he would have to leave a message, delaying information and increasing his tension.

"Detective Morrison."

Pete blew out a relieved breath upon hearing the detective's voice. "Hi, Detective Morrison," Pete responded. "This is Pete. Uh, I got your text." Then he hit the speaker button and added, "I'm here with Vincentius and a few others. You're on speaker."

"Thank you for getting back to me, Pete," Detective Morrison replied. To Pete's ear, he sounded frustrated with something. "I'm really sorry about this. I just found out about Winston today. He was released last week."

"How the hell did that asshole make parole?" Thad snarled, stalking into the room with Lachlan behind him. His hazel eyes narrowed as he took in Pete and Austin's positions, but he didn't say anything. Instead, Thad settled on a sofa nearby and rested his forearms on his thighs while glaring at the phone. "He wasn't supposed to get out for another ten years, at least."

Thad had been one of the men who'd stopped Winston and Leeson from hurting Pete that day. Pete would be forever grateful for their appearance. They'd also become amazing friends over the last several years.

"Thought you were still at the reception," Ashton murmured softly, eyeing Thad. "You weren't at the table when it all went down."

Pete knew Thad and Lachlan had been chatting with a few other enforcers instead of eating with them.

"Saw you leave, so I asked the guys what was going on," Thad revealed. "Followed you as quickly as we could."

Lachlan settled on the sofa, handing Thad a glass of red wine — probably a cab — while holding a tumbler filled with an amber liquid.

"Well, according to the paperwork I pulled" — Detective Morrison's voice drew everyone's attention — "Winston was a model inmate, and when overcrowding forced the release of a few people, Winston was one of the guys chosen." Even as several men growled their obvious anger, Detective Morrison hurried to continue, "So far, he's made all his check-ins with his parole officer. Plus, there's a restraining order against him. He's not to get within fifty yards of you, Pete."

"That's something, at least," Vincentius grumbled, clearly displeased.

"If the man is smart, he'll take his second chance to heart and not bother you," the detective added.

"Yeah, right," Lachlan muttered under his breath. "I've seen way too many of those types to think that's possible."

Detective Morrison's deep sigh came through the line. "I know what you're thinking. That's why I let Pete know as soon as I found out. If you see anything, hear anything from him, contact me immediately."

"I will," Pete assured even as the hairs on his nape stood on end. After a second of hesitation, he added, "Thank you for the heads up, Detective."

"You're welcome, Pete," the detective replied. "And I'm

truly sorry."

After the line disconnected, Pete whispered, "Me, too."

The group sat in silence for a few seconds, their expressions ranging from anger to frustration to disbelief.

Suddenly, Cho bounced from his seat. "I'm going to do some digging," he claimed. "Set up some stuff to keep an eye on Winston."

"Good idea." Vincentius also rose. His eyes were narrowed, determination filling his expression as he stared at Pete. "If he has any designs on coming after you, we'll know soon enough."

Pete nodded, staying silent. He didn't really know what to say. Instead, he cuddled into the huge man holding him, grateful to have so many people in his corner.

CHAPTER FIVE

A s soon as Vincentius and Cho disappeared, Austin found himself pinned under Thad's hazel-eyed gaze. His lips were pressed into a thin line. His frown and the way he raked his attention over Austin told him this was the shifter who planned to interrogate him.

Austin also found that he didn't mind. He appreciated that someone had Pete's back.

"Let's get to the meat of the potatoes. So, you're claiming to be Pete's mate," Thad stated coolly, his slight botching of a familiar expression distracting Austin for an instant before the other shifter continued talking. "I've seen you in the house before, Austin. Why didn't you say anything before?"

With a shrug, Austin replied, "Pete is my mate, Thad."

Austin knew the wild turkey shifter acted as the flock's enforcer while Ashton was their alpha. They'd integrated into Vincentius's household when Cho had mated with the councilman. The beta was a raven shifter named Gilbert who'd mated with Hess.

They were unique. Somehow, they continued their tiny little shifter flock dynamics while living within the councilman's household. Austin didn't know how, but it seemed to work for them.

"I don't know how I haven't run across him here before now." Austin sure wished he'd had his mate's support over the last year, but—"Everything works in Fate's time. Not our own, even if we wish it would." Nuzzling Pete's temple, Austin added, "But we've found each other now, and that's all that matters. I won't let anything happen to the other half of my soul, my perfect gift."

"Huh." Thad crossed his arms over his chest. "You okay there, Pete?"

Pete opened his mouth once, then closed it again. Turning his head, he smiled up at Austin before addressing Thad. "You know, I really am." He waved toward Austin. "About this anyway." Sighing, he shook his head. "Can't say I'm okay about the whole Winston thing, but that's totally out of my hands. Ya know?"

"Shoulda extracted shifter justice when we had the chance," Thad grumbled.

"That wasn't your call," Lachlan claimed, rubbing Thad's back. "That was between Pete and Vincentius."

Recalling something similar had been mentioned before, Austin asked, "What are you guys talking about? I thought you stopped Winston from" — he hesitated but forced himself to continue — "from raping Pete. Did that happen here on the councilman's property?"

Lachlan shook his head. "No, it happened at the botanical gardens," he revealed. "They took off before the cops got there, so the detective put a warrant out for both Winston and Leeson." Shaking his head, Lachlan explained, "The next day, they showed up with a bunch of rogue shifters who'd been tracking me. When Bashir read their memories, they'd overheard one of the shifters talking about sneaking onto Vincentius's estate. They asked the rogues to take them, too, because of their unfinished business with Pete." Shrugging, Lachlan rolled his eyes and sneered. "Of course, rogues don't mind using moronic humans as fodder, so they agreed. They didn't know about paranormals until Thad and another guy fought in shifted form." With a heated smile at his mate, Lachlan boasted, "My mate won, of course."

Nodding slowly, Austin could imagine the scene. Bashir

was a vampire under Vincentius's employ. "So, Bashir wiped their memories of the paranormal aspect and turned the pair over to the police, adding the charge of attempted kidnapping."

"Exactly," Lachlan confirmed.

"It's possible Winston really did learn his lesson," Pete murmured. While his mate's tone sounded uncertain, his scent screamed of hope, fear, and worry. "Maybe he really will just let it go."

Austin rubbed his hand up and down Pete's side, enjoying the feel of his lean, toned flesh beneath the clothes. "Maybe, babe." While Austin didn't really believe that, he wanted to reassure his mate, too. "And if Winston decides to do something stupid, we'll deal with it the shifter way, this time."

"What does that mean?" Pete asked, glancing between them.

"There's no three strikes in our world, Pete," Lachlan explained softly. "We gave him his one out. If he doesn't change from that, he'll be put down like any rogue shifter."

Austin felt a shudder work through Pete even as he mumbled, "Oh." His mate grimaced while nodding. "Okay."

After that, there wasn't much else to say on the matter. Once they had information from Cho or Vincentius, they could lay in a course of action. As it was, Austin just wanted to get Pete somewhere comfortable where he could relax and unwind.

Maybe explore every inch of his delectable body in the process.

Austin could think of all kinds of ways to help his mate relax. Those ideas had a predictable reaction on his body. His blood heated and flowed south. His prick began to swell in anticipation.

"Do you plan to bond with Pete right away?" Thad asked bluntly. He sniffed the air pointedly. "You recall he's human, right? He may like a little time to get to know you first."

With a huff, Pete raised his hand. "Human sitting right

here." The move adjusted his position, which caused his ass to press even tighter against Austin's quickly thickening dick. Obviously, Pete felt it, for his eyes widened, and he snapped his attention to Austin. "Oh."

"Yeah, oh," Thad quipped dryly. "Well, Austin?"

"That's between me and Pete," Austin countered, holding his mate's gaze. "I'll give you as much time as you need, but never doubt that I do want you." Running his palm over Pete's shoulder and down his arm, Austin claimed, "You are delectable, and I want to kiss every inch of your body." Reining in his need, he quickly added, "But it'll happen on your timetable. Not mine."

Pete licked his lips, then nibbled his bottom one. His brows furrowed a smidge. He looked for all the world as if he were thinking hard.

The move also drew Austin's attention to Pete's lips. He wanted to replace his mate's teeth with his own. He would suck and nibble that plump flesh to his heart's content. He wanted to —

A low chuckle yanked Austin out of his lustful thoughts, which was probably a good thing. He'd begun to scent Pete's own exotic scent of need, telling him that his mate was getting turned on. He didn't know if it was the way Austin continued to rub over his arm and shoulder or if it was the expression on Austin's own face, but his sexy mate was not unaffected.

However, they did still need to talk. Plus, they weren't alone in the room.

"So, yes," Austin began slowly. "Patience is difficult when a shifter finds his mate, but that doesn't mean we can't give it." Teasing a fingertip down Pete's jaw, Austin smiled at him. "Will you talk to me, my mate? Will you share your thoughts about our relationship?"

Pete inhaled deeply. He let it out just as slowly, then nodded. "Um, I've been around paranormals long enough to know that you all do things fast." He scoffed softly as he continued, "Like, moving in together within days fast." Peering at Austin from beneath his lashes, he whispered, "But I'd really like to go on a date with my boyfriend before anything like that happens."

Austin nodded once. While waiting would be difficult — and would hurt — for his mate, he would do it. "Then I shall take you out." With a wink, he asked, "Are you available this evening?"

With the wedding having taken place in the early afternoon, there was still plenty of the day left.

To Austin's relief, Pete chuckled softly. "As a matter of fact, I am."

"Dinner and a movie," Austin announced, the idea popping into his head. "How does that sound?"

Pete nodded. "Okay. When?"

Humming, Austin pulled out his phone so he could check the time. As soon as he woke his device, Bran's contact information appeared on the screen. Recalling that had been the last thing he'd been looking at before getting ready for the wedding, Austin felt his arousal die a quick death.

"Hey, are you okay?" Pete rested his hand over Austin's wrist, squeezing lightly. Evidently, he was staring at the screen, too, for he asked, "Who's Bran?"

Austin swallowed hard, trying to get some moisture into his suddenly too-dry throat. "My brother," he answered roughly. "I-I need to call him. I've been putting it off. He n-needs to know — "

Pausing, Austin felt a fresh wave of anguish stab through his chest.

As if sensing his pain, Pete rubbed over his pectorals, petting him, soothing him. "Know what?" When Austin met Pete's gaze, he must have read something in his eyes, for he told him, "If you're not ready to tell me, you don't have to."

Austin sighed as he refocused on his phone. "It's not a secret," he managed to whisper huskily. "Just painful."

"Pete," Lachlan called softly. "Austin's brothers went rogue with the ex-councilmen. They were—" He ended the sentence on a grunt, his meaning clear.

They were put down.

"Oh," Pete breathed the word on a soft sigh. He continued rubbing Austin's chest. "Were you close?"

Austin shook his head. "No, but that just makes it worse, you know?"

Pete frowned. "How so?"

"If I *had* been close to them"—Austin met Pete's questioning gaze, peering into his beautiful brown eyes—"maybe I would have noticed the signs that they were thinking of doing something stupid. Maybe I could have stopped them."

"Or, maybe they would have dragged you down with them," Pete countered, his tone sympathetic. "Or maybe they would have ignored you. Or maybe they were so good at hiding what they were preparing to do that you wouldn't have noticed anything anyway." With a shrug, Pete added, "I hear things hiding under the hood of a car all day. People walk in and out of the garage, their phones attached to their ears, and they never stop to think about the guy under the car." With a sympathetic smile, Pete told him, "If I got a dollar every time I heard someone say, I can't believe I didn't notice anything about so-and-so or such-and-such, I'd be rich."

Austin continued to stare, uncertain how to respond.

Pete squeezed his wrist lightly and told him, "I guess what I'm trying to say is, you can't take the blame for someone else's mistakes. They made their choice. That's on them."

Something tight unfurled within Austin's chest. It was something he hadn't even realized had been there.

Guilt.

He'd been carrying around so much guilt about failing his brothers. While it wasn't gone completely, it had eased. His breathing came a little easier, and his heart warmed for the sweet, small human sitting on his lap.

"Thank you," Austin murmured. He indicated his phone, noticing the time on it. "And how about we check movies and decide when to leave based on that?"

Pete smiled up at him. "Sounds good." Then he focused on the phone again. "Would you like me to leave, so you can call your brother?"

Austin immediately shook his head. "Actually, I'd like you to stay." Grimacing, he admitted, "I can't even say that he'll pick up if he knows that it's me calling. He stopped returning my letters over fifty years ago."

Wincing in sympathy, Pete shook his head. "I'm sorry."

Austin tightened the arm he had around Pete's waist, taking comfort in having his mate with him. "I apologize ahead of time if there's yelling or cussing."

Pete smirked as he rolled his eyes. "Mechanic, remember?" He pointed to his own chest. "I can cuss with the best of them. Especially when I cut myself on a piece of metal or get sprayed by some nasty fluid."

Smiling, Austin nodded. "Had those things happen plenty of times. I get it." Then he bit the bullet and pressed the call button on Bran's contact.

The phone rang once, twice, before it was picked up. "Hello?" The deep voice on the other end sounded a little wary.

It also caused Austin's breath to catch in his throat. He hadn't heard Bran's voice in over eighty years, but he still recognized it. Opening his mouth, Austin tried to speak, but he couldn't manage to form words.

"Hello?"

Pete must have noticed his predicament, for he hit the speaker button on the phone before saying, "Um, hi. My name is Pete." He stared at Austin as he added, "I'm looking for

Bran. Is that you?"

"Yeah, I'm Bran." The man didn't say more.

"Well, um, I'm here with your brother. Austin," Pete revealed.

That provoked a reaction.

"I don't have anything to say to that deserter."

"Wait, please don't hang up," Pete cried. "Please, wait."

"Why should I?" Bran demanded.

Finally, Austin managed to unglue his tongue from the roof of his mouth. "It's about Gaston and Ephram."

"I don't have anything to say to them, either," Bran claimed belligerently. "You're all dead to me."

"They *are* dead," Austin blurted. "They went rogue, and they were put down for their crimes."

The sound of Bran sucking in a harsh breath filled the line. Then, for several seconds, there was silence. "Rogue?" he whispered. "What the hell happened?"

Austin blew out a heavy breath. "Have you heard about the changes going on in the council? The turnover due to the crimes a couple of councilmen have committed?"

"I'm not in the inner circle," Bran admitted. "So all I've heard is rumors about how they're letting councilmen be fags and lie about fated mates."

Austin winced at Bran's choice of words while exchanging a look with Pete. He knew his mate was just as concerned. Having not seen Bran in over eighty years and not communicated with him in over fifty, Austin didn't know if that attitude was a recent development or not.

"Two councilmen were found guilty of selling shifters to scientists to be experimented on," Austin explained slowly, choosing his words carefully. "That's why they were removed, but they didn't like losing their power, so they went rogue, taking a few council enforcers with them, Gaston and Ephram included." With a sigh, Austin told his brother,

"That's why they were executed. They tried to attack a councilman that was out for a run with his mate. A male mate." Holding Pete's gaze, Austin finished with, "And the fact that Fate does pair those of the same sex is not a lie. It's the truth. It really does happen. In fact, it's even happened to me. Pete is my fated mate."

CHAPTER SIX

"You're shitting me."

Pete still chuckled upon thinking of Bran's response. He knew Austin had been surprised that his brother hadn't hung up on them. In fact, they'd enjoyed their drinks and talked to Bran for over an hour.

They had even made plans to talk in a few days.

"That's not how I thought that would go," Austin admitted, his quiet voice rumbling a little in wonder. He stared at his phone as if he couldn't believe the last hour had happened. "Bran talked to me. He didn't blame me."

"That's because it wasn't your fault," Pete insisted. He pointed at their empty beer bottle and wine glass. "Refill?"

Austin hummed, then nodded. "As long as I still get to hold you while drinking it." He tightened his grip, not allowing Pete to move until he'd agreed.

Pete chuckled softly as he slipped off Austin's lap. He picked up both items. The bottle he placed in the recycle bin. The glass he put on the sideboard to be used again. After filling his glass, Pete fished out a fresh bottle for Austin.

Returning to Austin, Pete admired his soon-to-be lover's rugged features. He didn't kid himself. He wouldn't be able to resist Austin for long. The man was just too fine, too kind, and the draw was magnetic.

The more time Pete spent in Austin's company, the more he understood why couples turned their lives upside down so swiftly.

"Here ya go." Pete handed the bottle to Austin, who then

46

helped him back onto his lap.

"May I kiss you as a thank you?" Austin asked, surprising him.

Pete hesitated only an instant before he nodded. "Yes, you may."

Austin lifted his free hand and gently cradled Pete's jaw. While skimming his thumb under Pete's lower lip, he dipped his head. Ever-so-lightly, Austin pressed his mouth to Pete's in a gentle kiss so full of reverence that it caused his gut to clench.

When Austin drew away, he smiled at Pete. His dark eyes gleamed with happiness. He even parted his lips on a sigh, as if that had been the most amazing kiss of his life.

"Wow," Pete whispered, expressing his own pleasure at the experience.

Smiling wider, Austin lowered his hand to Pete's side. "Your mouth is a thing of beauty," he rumbled with obvious happiness. Then he cleared his throat and turned his attention to his phone. "So, times a-wasting. Let's see what's in the theaters."

They spent the next ten minutes scrolling through theater listings and weighing the pros and cons of certain movies. They finally decided on an action-comedy flick. They bought tickets online before picking out a restaurant near the cinema.

"I'm going to go grab my bag from the car," Austin told him. "I know there's a powder room around the corner. I'm going to change in there and get cleaned up a little. Meet me back here in fifteen?"

Pete nodded happily. "Sounds good."

Austin once again cradled Pete's jaw. He dipped his head once more, sealing their lips together. The huge man gently lapped across Pete's lower lip, but when Pete parted them, he didn't take advantage. Instead, Austin gently suckled his bottom lip for a few seconds before nipping it lightly and drawing away.

Sighing, Austin muttered, "I'm going to get addicted to your lips." The corners of his mouth quirked. "Delicious."

Feeling as if his heart skipped a beat in his chest, Pete could only think of one thing to say. "I wouldn't have a problem with that."

"Good." Austin eased to his feet, allowing Pete to slide off his thighs. "See you in a minute."

Pete stared as Austin walked away. His attention lowered to the huge man's rock-hard ass as he moved, the globes flexing beneath the fabric of his jeans. He clenched his hands, wondering how those globes would feel in his palms.

Magnificent, I bet.

It wasn't until Austin had disappeared that Pete shook himself out of his lustful thoughts and started to his own bedroom.

When Pete reached his door, a grinning Prescott waited. "Congrats on finding your mate," the wood duck shifter offered. "Heard you were going on a date tonight."

"Uh, yeah," Pete replied, heading inside.

Prescott followed without an invitation, but that wasn't anything new. They were all pretty open about their space unless they were with their significant others. Then they always knocked.

Pete didn't know when Prescott and his mate, Nkosi, had gotten home, but he figured he'd heard about his upcoming date from Thad and Lachlan. Pete had noticed the pair slip out of the room right before Austin had called his brother.

"Um, so what are you doing here?" Pete asked, crossing to his closet.

"Helping you pick out an outfit," Prescott answered as if that was a given. He tapped his chin and hummed as he began moving around the shirts in his closet. Prescott was frowning. "Um, do you have anything"—he waved his hand as if searching for the right word — "dressy other than that?"

Prescott pointed at the nice clothes Pete had specifically purchased for Dane and Danny's wedding.

Scoffing, Pete shook his head. "Sorry, Pres. I'm a mechanic. I live in jeans, tees, and coveralls."

Shaking his head, Prescott eyed him up and down. "I think some of Hector's clothes might fit you." He began hurrying out of the room, calling over his shoulder, "Be right back."

Pete shook his head as he hollered back, "Nothing too fancy. It's just dinner and a movie."

Prescott paused for just a few seconds to give him an in-credulous look before continuing from the room.

Shrugging, Pete kicked off his shoes and placed them aside. He quickly stripped and headed into the bathroom. Without knowing how long Prescott would be, Pete made quick work of washing himself down to remove any sweat from his mild freak-outs of the day — from meeting Austin to discovering Winston was free.

Damn. Did I really only meet Austin a few hours ago? I feel like I've known him forever.

Pete accepted it, though. He'd seen it happen with count-less other people.

And now, it's my turn.

Smiling to himself, Pete pulled on a pair of silk boy-shorts underwear — his guilty pleasure. He rolled on a fresh coat of deodorant before grabbing his favorite jeans, ones that he knew cradled his ass to perfection. Then he started flipping through his shirts.

Sadly, Prescott was right. He really didn't have much in the *nice for a date* category. Just as he began to run his fingers through his hair in uncertainty, Prescott came sweeping back in.

The shifter eyed his jeans, then jerked a nod in obvious ap-proval. That was good because no way was he stripping back to his underwear in front of the man. He knew shifters weren't shy, most having to get naked to change forms or risk destroying their clothes or getting stuck. That didn't mean Pete was willing to show Prescott his underwear. That was private.

But I'd be willing to show Austin.

Thoughts of how Austin would react to them sent a surge of nerves through him.

What if he doesn't like them?

"Here." Prescott held a shirt out to him. "And I don't know what you're thinking about, but this is your mate we're talking about. Whatever it is, it'll be fine."

Pete appreciated the support even as he was relieved Prescott didn't press him for his thoughts. Taking the shirt, he held it up and arched one eyebrow. The fabric was sheer with a metallic sheen to it.

Handing it back, Pete shook his head. "Nope. We're not going clubbing." When Prescott refused to take it, Pete dropped it on the bed and crossed his arms over his chest. "What else ya got?"

Even as Prescott heaved a put-upon sigh, he turned back to the other items he'd draped over the back of a chair. He flipped through them for a few seconds before pulling out another one.

Pete took it, pleased with the second choice. He tugged the green polo shirt over his head. It fitted to his body without appearing painted on as if it were too tight or too small.

"Oh, yeah," Prescott murmured, nodding. "Perfect. It even brings out the green flecks in your eyes."

Cocking his head, Pete asked, "I have green flecks in my eyes?" He'd always considered his brown eyes boring.

Prescott nodded widely. "Yup. They're pretty." Clapping his hands, he looked him up and down. "I called Cho to bring you his dress boots. Hurry and put on your socks."

Even as Pete obeyed, he admitted, "I was just gonna wear my sneakers."

Shaking his head, Prescott told him, "No, no. Not for your first date."

There was a perfunctory knock on the door before Cho came striding in. He wore only a sarong, and his hair was mussed. The way his skin glowed and how his lips were plumped gave him a distinctively just-fucked look.

The beaming smile on his face was a dead giveaway, too.

"Oh, you look hot," Cho claimed, setting his boots on the floor. "Austin isn't gonna be able to keep his hands off of you."

Pete didn't point out that that seemed to already be the case. Instead, he smiled and thanked the guys. After tugging on Cho's low-heeled dress boots, he had to admit that they did complete the outfit.

Glancing at the clock, Pete realized his time was up just as Prescott ordered, "Come into the bathroom. I'll style your hair."

Laughing, Pete shook his head. "I gotta go. My hair is fine." As he grabbed a light jacket, phone, and keys, he added, "Besides, hopefully, we'll be running our fingers through each other's hair soon, so styling it further would be a waste."

Plus, Pete kept his hair short for a reason. He didn't like having to do much with it. Working in the garage, he would get hot and sweaty, and if it was too long, it would flop in his face.

So much easier just to have it short enough to be caught by a bandana.

Even as Prescott called, "Wait," Cho was laughing and shouting, "Good luck!"

"Thanks, guys." Pete waved and left them in his room.

Hurrying to the front hall, Pete wondered if that was where he was supposed to meet Austin. They hadn't really discussed it. He figured if he didn't find him there, he would head to the powder room Austin had mentioned.

When Pete entered the hall, the sight of the formidable man

nearly took his breath away.

Austin had changed into a pair of relaxed-fit jeans. He still had on his nice dress boots. The dark top was half-hidden by his black leather jacket. Austin looked dashing and dangerous and oh-so-sexy.

"Oh, babe," Austin rumbled, stalking toward him. Heat gleamed in his dark eyes. "Not that you didn't look handsome before, but now . . . you look stunning."

As Austin reached for him, Pete managed to stutter out, "S-So do you."

Austin growled, "Thank you," before he cupped Pete's jaw and captured his lips.

Where Austin's past kisses had been gentle, sweet, and almost timid, this time, he thrust his tongue between Pete's lips and conquered. He lapped at his tongue, licking and gliding, learning his mouth.

Pete grabbed Austin's leather jacket and hung on for the ride. Never had he been kissed with, not aggression, really, but with passion, with need. As he worked hard to slide his tongue against Austin's and do a little exploring of his own, Pete's blood fired in his veins, rushing south.

His head swam, and his body erupted with heat. His cock throbbed behind his fly, and he moaned into Austin's mouth.

When Austin finally broke the kiss, Pete trembled while sucking in a deep breath of air.

"Damn, Pete," Austin rumbled, hauling him in close. With his arms wrapped tightly around Pete, Austin rubbed up and down his back soothingly. "Gods, babe. Didn't mean to maul you like that." His voice came out rough with want and need. "You just looked so edible. Needed a taste."

Still clinging to Austin's jacket, Pete rested heavily against the much-larger man. He panted, trying to catch his breath. He shivered as his dick twitched in time with his heartbeats.

"You okay, my mate?"

Austin's worried voice cut through the fog in Pete's head.

Tipping his head back, Pete peered up at Austin's face. He saw the worry, the concern etched across his features. Knowing he needed to ease that, Pete smiled and forced his sluggish brain to form words.

"I-I'm okay," Pete assured. "Never had" — he paused to clear his throat — "never had anyone kiss me like that. Wow." After a couple of heartbeats, where Austin seemed to be searching his features, Pete assured, "I loved it. M-Maybe next time, um, we can do that somewhere private?"

Groaning softly, Austin nodded. "Hell, yeah." The worry eased from his eyes, and he smiled down at him. "Ready for dinner and a movie?"

Even as his dick twitched, as if saying no, Pete nodded. "Yes. Let's go."

Austin eased his hold slowly, perhaps to make certain Pete was steady on his feet. Keeping one arm around his waist, he guided Pete to the garage and back into his *Stingray*.

Without the duffle bag and boots taking up space, Pete relaxed in the seat and willed his erection to ease up.

CHAPTER SEVEN

Releasing Pete so they could go on their date had been one of the hardest things Austin had ever needed to do in his life. The scent of his mate's arousal — so thick and potent — had called to his basest of instincts. He'd wanted to find the nearest flat surface and pleasure his mate until they were both sweaty and sated, unable to walk.

Unfortunately, Austin knew that couldn't happen. He'd reined in his raging need by sheer force of will alone. Feeling his mate, his soon-to-be lover, trembling against him, his erection pressed against his thigh, had been the most exquisite and most difficult thing to endure in his long life, knowing he couldn't do a damn thing about it, yet.

Austin took the short walk around the hood of his car to take several long, slow, deep breaths. He managed to regain some semblance of self-control by the time he eased into the driver's seat. Before bringing his *Corvette* to life, Austin reached over and squeezed Pete's hand.

"I'm looking forward to getting to know you better, my mate," Austin revealed.

"Same," Pete replied, smiling back at him.

With a swift nod, Austin started his car, then backed it out of the stall. As they cleared the bay door, rain pattered on the windows.

"It's beautiful."

Hearing Pete's softly spoken comment, Austin glanced at his mate. He saw the way he was peering up through the clear roof sections, taking in the night sky. Austin glanced up for a few heartbeats, taking in the storm overhead.

"Yes, it is," Austin agreed.

Under normal circumstances, Austin never would have driven his *Stingray* in the rain. He knew these weren't normal circumstances, however. The simple act of seeing the dark sky through raindrops seemed to please his mate, and he would do anything to please his mate.

Besides, the seals were tight, so no rain would get in the cab. He'd redone them all himself just a few years prior. Every time he washed the car, he verified that they still held.

And that had been just yesterday, so it would be clean to drive to the wedding.

Dismissing his concern for his car, Austin focused on the damp roads. He turned the radio on low, a station playing old country songs filling the cab with a Chris LeDoux ballad about a man and his hat. While Austin enjoyed the song, he still pointed and offered, "Want to find a channel?"

Pete shook his head and smiled at him. "I assume that if your radio was cued to this station, you like this music."

"I do," Austin confirmed, not at all shy about his preferences.

"Good." Pete turned in his seat and reached out, resting his hand on Austin's thigh. "Me, too."

Then Pete began to sing along with the radio.

Austin smiled and placed his palm over Pete's hand, squeezing lightly. He kept to the speed limit and relaxed, just enjoying the moment. While his dick threatened to thicken once more from the heat of Pete's palm, he would never remove it.

I have my mate, and we agree on music.

In Austin's book, the evening couldn't have started better.

The drive to the restaurant they'd chosen flew by way too swiftly. He was tempted to drive around the block just to extend the private moment. Hearing Pete's stomach rumble nixed that idea.

Austin parked his car and shut off the engine. After giving Pete's hand one more squeeze, he released him and unbuckled his belt. He noticed Pete did the same.

Once Austin exited the vehicle, he double-checked that Pete had locked his door. Then he did the same to his and closed it. He hurried around the hood as he shoved the keys into his pocket. Meeting his mate at the front of the car, Austin once again took his hand within his own, earning him a smile from his mate.

While Austin couldn't remember ever holding hands with anyone, he couldn't deny that it was quickly becoming one of his favorite things. There was just something so simple and wholesome about the activity. They were sharing skin, putting their scents on each other, and Austin knew it helped calm his beast, who would have been much happier to have their claiming mark on Pete before they'd walked out the door.

Patience. Soon. Gods, I hope soon.

Opening the door to the restaurant, Austin hurried Pete in out of the rain. He met the gaze of the hostess. "Two, please. Table, if possible."

While she scented of surprise, she nodded. "Of course, sir. This way, please." After picking up two menus, she led the way deeper into the establishment to a four-seater table on the right. "Here you are." She placed the menus opposite each other as she added, "Your server this evening is Mindy, and she'll be right out with your waters and silverware."

"Thank you," Pete responded, taking a seat.

Austin ignored the menu placement and settled to Pete's left. Then he slid the menu toward him, ignoring the surprised look on the woman's face.

Whatever.

Resting his right hand on the table, Austin gripped Pete's left hand.

Pete smiled and leaned close to whisper, "You're very

touchy-feely. I wouldn't have thought it."

"You're my mate, Pete," Austin responded, keeping his voice low. "We're not bonded yet, and we're out in public, so the need to touch is a little higher than normal." Realizing how that sounded — that he *wouldn't* feel the need to touch once they *were* bonded — Austin quickly corrected that notion by saying, "And I'll always want to touch you in some way. You're everything to me."

The glow in Pete's brown eyes appeared to intensify as his mate peered at him, making him even more handsome.

Spotting something, Austin leaned closer to Pete. "You know, you have gorgeous green flecks in your eyes." He barely resisted the urge to kiss his mate when he saw the adorable blush spread across his cheeks. "Stunning."

"Good evening, gentlemen." The friendly voice broke into their moment. "I'm Mindy, and I'll be your waitress this evening." As she continued speaking, she placed water glasses and napkin-wrapped silverware on the table. "Can I get you anything besides the water to drink? Are you interested in any appetizers? I can assure you that the lobster-stuffed mushrooms are amazing."

"Oh, no, thank you," Pete quickly replied. Then, as if he was worried he'd offended her, he added, "But how are your jalapeno poppers?"

Smiling widely at him, Mindy replied, "Another delicious option." She used a pen to point at the menu. "There's a sampler platter that contains them, along with potato skins and hot wing bites."

Pete's eyes lit up for an instant before dimming just as quickly. "Oh, well . . ."

Austin suddenly caught on to what Pete was looking at — the price.

Oh, hell, no.

"Absolutely." Austin lifted his gaze to Mindy. "We'll start with that." Then he pointed at another appetizer item. "And your bacon mac and cheese. The reviews say it's amazing."

Mindy's eyes widened, and she nodded quickly. "Oh, it is." With a hum, she scribbled on her order pad before adding, "I would eat that every day if it wouldn't ruin my girlish figure." She finished on a giggle while returning her gaze to them. "To drink?"

Recalling how Pete had enjoyed the glass of malbec at the councilman's house, he turned to the wine list. "Let's see," he began, scanning the options. "I'll take a bottle of this." He pointed at his choice.

Jotting it down, Mindy nodded once more. "Also yum." With another beaming smile, she told them, "I'll go get those started and be back with your wine."

Then Mindy hustled away.

Austin focused on Pete and saw him nibbling his bottom lip. "If you keep doing that, I'm going to want to replace your teeth with my own."

Pete's eyes widened, and confusion flooded his scent. "Huh?"

Chuckling softly, Austin indicated his bottom lip. "When you're worried or deep in thought, you nibble your bottom lip." He reached toward his mate and gently traced under it. "It makes me want to lick and suck it better."

As Austin had expected, Pete's face took on a pinkish hue.

With a smile, Austin winked, then returned his attention to his menu. "So, what's calling your name tonight? And are you not a fan of lobster?"

Shaking his head, Pete admitted, "No, not a fan of lobster. Or most fish, for that matter." He crinkled his nose in the most adorable fashion—not that Austin would ever tell his mate that—as he added, "Just something about the consistency. Makes me want—" Pete cut himself off, but Austin could guess at what he'd intended to say. "Well," Pete continued. "It just doesn't agree with me."

"Got it. No romantic steak and lobster dinners for us," Austin teased.

"Oh." Pete's eyes widened as he snapped his attention back to Austin. "You can eat it if you want. I don't mind that."

Austin reached over and gripped Pete's wrist, rubbing his thumb over his pulse point soothingly. "I'll keep it in mind." Then he returned his attention to his menu as he asked, "Anything you're allergic to?"

"Not that I've found so far."

"Good." Austin wouldn't want to make a meal that accidentally poisoned his mate. "Find what you want?"

"Mmmm, would it make me really boring to get this chipotle chicken wrap?"

Austin shook his head. "Not at all. I love chipotle."

"Well, I won't get it if you are," Pete countered. "I'll find something else, and we can share." Maybe thinking that was too forward, he quickly back-pedaled, "Unless you're not into that sort of thing?"

"First date?" Mindy asked, announcing her presence.

Nodding, Austin grinned at her. "It is, but it definitely won't be the last." He focused on Pete while keeping Mindy in his peripheral. "I mean, not only is Pete hot, but he's just as sweet and kind on the inside. I can't wait to learn all about him."

"Awww, that's so sweet," Mindy murmured as she opened the bottle of wine. "Either of you got a straight brother?"

Pete winced. "Uh, yeah, actually." Focusing on her, he admitted, "But he disowned me when I came out, so I wouldn't be able to hook you up. Sorry."

Mindy's eyes widened, then narrowed. "Well, I wouldn't want a bigot anyway. My sister is a lesbian." Clearing her expression just as fast, she indicated the wine. "Who's going to try it?"

Austin indicated Pete. "Give it a shot, babe. Tell me what

you think."

After Pete had tried it and confirmed that he liked it, Mindy began pouring more wine.

While she did, Austin admitted, "I was estranged from my brother for a few years" — more than, not that he could tell her that—"but if he turns out to be a good guy, I'll keep you in mind."

Mindy snickered as she caught the wine drip. "You guys are too kind." After placing the bottle on the table, she straightened. "Are you ready to order? Or do you need another minute?"

When Austin saw Pete hesitate, he replied, "Another minute, please."

"I'll be back in a few to check on you," Mindy promised before heading away.

"She's cute," Pete commented, watching the vivacious and friendly blonde make her way from one table to the next. "Did Bran have a type back in the day?"

Austin shrugged. "Not a clue."

"Do you think he'll come visit, or you go to visit him?" Pete seemed to ask the question absently, his attention returning to the menu.

Humming, Austin gave it the thought it was due. "I'm not certain I'd want to deal with the herd's alpha, considering some of the comments Bran made." The alpha had sounded like a bigoted asshole, and Austin bet the man was still just as controlling as ever. "Maybe we can convince him to come visit. Or meet us at the cabin." Realizing he was making assumptions, Austin asked, "Would you be interested in going to the cabin with me soon? I have two weeks off, so maybe next week?"

At first, Pete looked like he was going to agree. His eyes lit up, and he opened his mouth. Then he grimaced and shook his head.

"I really do have a lot of work stacked up, and I just agreed to take in an SUV for Germaine."

"You know, I'm not a bad mechanic myself," Austin told him. "Not to brag, but I *did* do all the work on my *Stingray*. Maybe I can help you get ahead?"

Pete stared at him with wide eyes. "I can't ask you to work on your vacation."

"You didn't ask. I offered," Austin pointed out. Leaning closer to Pete, he lowered his voice and added, "Besides, spending every waking moment with my newly discovered mate, helping him get everything together so we can run away together for a few days?" His expression grew heated. "My dear mate, that is *not* a hardship. Not at all."

"O-Okay." Pete's smile appeared a little uncertain, but he was agreeing. "I think that would be fun. I haven't been out of the city in"—with a shake of his head, he admitted—"I don't know how long."

"Good. Then it's settled." Austin leaned over and pecked a kiss to Pete's temple. "We'll wrap up things with your work and run away together."

When Austin straightened, he saw Pete's wide-eyed look and the pink staining his cheeks. He realized it must have been the kiss and vowed to do whatever was necessary to help Pete see how much he meant to him. His mate deserved just as much happiness as Austin could manage to give him.

Pete took a sip of his wine, eyeing Austin over the rim of his glass, perhaps to buy a few seconds to compose himself.

Austin didn't comment. Instead, he returned his attention to the menu as he urged, "Get the chipotle wrap you want. I think this three-cheese chicken and shrimp pasta dish is calling my name."

CHAPTER EIGHT

About thirty minutes into the movie, Pete realized he'd lost the plot. He was sure it was a good movie, but he just couldn't concentrate on it. Instead, all his focus was on Austin's heated body curled up beside his own.

The cinema was only a few years old, and they'd installed some pretty nice features. Upon entering, Austin had chosen seats near the back, isolating them from the few other viewers. He'd flipped up the armrest between their chairs. Finally, Austin had reclined their chairs a little ways, then tugged Pete into his arms, cradling him against his body.

Pete's head rested on Austin's shoulder. He had his arm draped over his expansive torso, and their hips were pressed close. Never would he have expected the big shifter to be a cuddler, but there they were.

It was damn distracting.

With his thoughts drifting to all the things Pete wanted to do to the man beside him, he accepted that the movie was a lost cause. That didn't mean the evening was a bust, however. Instead, Pete began a slow exploration of Austin's chest through the material of his shirt.

Pete traced the lines of his pectorals. Then he felt out the ridges of his abdominals, counting. He had to do it a second time to be sure.

Yup, he's got an eight-pack. Wow!

Austin growled softly into his ear. His warm breath ghosted over the fine hairs of his neck when he whispered, "The movie not to your liking?"

"The movie's fine," Pete whispered back absently, spotting the large bulge behind Austin's fly. *Oh, wow.* After a quick peek around, making sure there was no one close — *nope, the closest people are a couple of guys eight rows up and quite a bit to the right* — Pete asked, "Can I have your jacket, please?"

"You cold, my mate?" Austin asked quietly, even as he reached to his left and grabbed his leather jacket.

As Pete took it and awkwardly began to spread it over their laps, he admitted, "Not really."

"Then what is it?" Still, Austin helped him spread it over them.

"Just wanted to touch," Pete replied, relaxing against Austin once more, returning his hand to Austin's stomach.

Austin's chuckle sounded a little rough to Pete's ears. "You are touching, and it's making it very difficult to be good."

Pete felt Austin's hand twitch on his thigh, as if struggling to keep it still. The arm around his back tightened, as did those fingers on his hip. Smiling, Pete hoped his big date wouldn't stop him from what he had planned next.

"I don't want you to be good," Pete admitted as he skimmed his hand down Austin's stomach to his groin. He felt the hard ridge trapped beneath the fly just as Austin sucked in a sharp breath.

"Pete," Austin hissed. "What are you doing?"

"This."

Feeling over Austin's erection, Pete traced the thick slab of man-meat. *Yum!* He located the big man's fly and slowly, carefully, eased down the zipper. Then he teased his fingertips inside.

Score!

Just as Pete had hoped, as a shifter, Austin didn't wear underwear. He was immediately able to feel the satiny steel flesh of the man's erection. While Pete felt Austin tense beside him and his breathing picked up, he didn't say anything or make a move to stop him.

Under the cover of the leather jacket, Pete used his thumb to pop the button on his jeans. Immediately, as if it had a mind of its own, Austin's cock pressed into his hand. Pete immediately wrapped his hand around it, his fingers barely touching due to Austin being so thick.

Moving slowly, Pete began jacking Austin's dick. He took his time, tracing the pulsing veins running its length. Pausing at the top, he massaged the wrinkled skin beneath the thickly flared head before swiping over his crown, finding it wet with pre-cum.

"Fuck," Austin hissed before tucking his face and pressing it to Pete's neck. "Gods, baby." His words barely reached Pete over the sounds of the explosions on-screen. "Please, don't stop."

Pete obeyed, pleased to have Austin's permission. He fondled every inch of his shifter's erection, and there was a lot of it. Using the man's pre-cum helped ease his way a bit, and when he reached the base, he dipped into his jeans and cradled his balls.

Austin whined where his face was pressed against Pete's neck. He lifted his hips, allowing Pete to push his jeans down a smidge so he could draw out his testicles. His warm breath huffed against Pete's neck, betraying how swiftly he panted.

After one more gentle roll to his sack, Pete returned his hand to Austin's shaft. He squeezed and tugged, massaged and swiped, doing all the things he liked to do to his own cock. Keeping his movements purposefully slow, Pete did his best to draw out his lover's pleasure, and never once did Austin complain, lying there and taking it, seeming to enjoy every second of it.

Pete wasn't certain how long he enjoyed groping Austin before the man whined, "C-Close."

For an instant, Pete froze, realizing they were probably about to make one hell of a mess. Then he remembered he'd been wearing his jacket in the garage the prior day when he'd been discussing a repair with Seever. He'd grabbed a shop towel to wipe some dirt off of the SUV he'd just washed, uncertain how he'd missed it, then shoved the towel into his jacket pocket.

"Just a sec," Pete murmured, releasing Austin's dick. He smirked upon hearing the slight whine but didn't comment on it. He turned and yanked the towel out of his jacket pocket, then slipped it and his arm back under Austin's leather jacket.

Pete draped the towel over Austin's dick by feel before gripping his shifter's length once more. Resuming his ministrations, he picked up his pace just a little. Hearing Austin's quiet moan, feeling him jolt against him as his erection erupted in his grip, filled Pete with pride.

I did that. I pleased him so much that he lost all control in the back of a movie theater.

Slowing his movements, Pete did his best to extend Austin's pleasure. He felt the wetness of the towel on the backs of his fingers as he continued to touch and tease. Finally, Austin moved his hand from his thigh to grip Pete's wrist, stalling his movements.

"Oh, fuck, babe," Austin muttered, lifting his head to peer down at him. His smile appeared a little loopy, and his eyes glittered with satiation in the light from the movie screen. "That was amazing. *You* are amazing." Then his eyes narrowed, and he growled, "My turn."

Austin captured Pete's mouth in a slow, sensuous kiss. His tongue slipped into his mouth and teased over every inch. He lifted the hand from Pete's hip and moved it up his back to thread into his hair, using the hold to get his mouth at just the right angle.

As Austin plundered his mouth, dipping his tongue into him over and over in a parody of sex, he released Pete's wrist. He pressed his hand over Pete's rock-hard cock and squeezed through the fabric. When Pete fed him a moan, he drank it down, the noise masked by the movie.

Austin made quick work of Pete's fly, exposing his satin boy shorts to his talented fingers. He broke the kiss just long enough to murmur, "Sexy. Can't wait to see these later." Then he started to kiss Pete once more.

When Pete felt his underwear pushed down, he felt the unmistakable feel of a slightly damp cloth pushed over his sensitive crown. Austin's calloused hand wrapped around his length and began a swift jacking. Pete felt his balls tighten almost immediately. He'd been on the edge too long. Teasing Austin had been the hottest thing he could ever remember doing.

If Pete hadn't been so out of his mind with arousal, he would have felt embarrassed at how swiftly he came. After only a handful of tugs, his testicles burst. His cock erupted in spurt after spurt of seed as the most exquisite release sent his senses soaring.

Unable to help himself, Pete moaned. Fortunately, Austin muffled it with his own lips as he continued to tease him through several more spine-tingling bursts.

Finally, when the need to breathe became too much to ignore, Pete turned his head and broke the kiss. It was Pete's turn to tuck his face against Austin's neck. He panted harshly, trying to catch his breath after experiencing the greatest ecstasy of his life.

And from a hand job!

After a few moments, Pete became aware of Austin's quiet hums as he nuzzled his goatee against his temple. His big lover held him close, safe in his arms, as he floated back to himself. With a soft sigh, Pete relaxed in his man's embrace.

They rested that way for a while, their faces pressed together, neither seeming to care about the movie.

Eventually, a low husky chuckle vibrated through Austin's chest. "Damn, babe," he murmured into his ear. "That was. Ha. So fucking hot."

Pete eased his face back a couple of inches so he could meet Austin's gaze. "Despite where we are?"

Austin smirked, his gaze heavy-lidded. "That just made it hotter." Then he winked and told him, "Don't worry. Shifter hearing let me keep track of what others were doing. No one noticed."

"Good." Pete felt himself blushing. "Don't want to get into trouble." Then he grimaced. "Or traumatize anyone."

"We didn't," Austin assured. "You ready to straighten up a little?" He glanced toward the screen and cocked his head. "I think we have another twenty-thirty minutes to the show."

Pete nodded. "Yeah."

With slow, careful movements, they both righted their clothes under the cover of Austin's large jacket. Pete carefully folded the cum-filled towel and tucked it into his own jacket's pocket. He made a mental note to add both items to his laundry.

Once they were both tucked away, buttoned and zipped, Austin cuddled Pete back to his chest. He sighed, pressed a kiss to Pete's cheek, then relaxed once more.

To Pete's surprise, even after his epic release, his dick didn't soften to less than half-mast.

Huh. Must be a shifter mate thing.

Once the movie ended, they righted their seats, picked up their jackets, and headed out of the theater.

Pete cast discreetly about, but he didn't notice anyone paying them any mind. Instead, the few other people who'd been in there seemed to be focused on rehashing their favorite parts of the movie. If Pete could remember most of it, perhaps he and Austin would be doing the same.

With no one the wiser, Pete slid his hand into Austin's, earning him a smile, and they exited the theater.

As they made their way to Austin's *Corvette*, Pete took in a deep breath of the fresh evening air. The rain had tapered off, leaving the evening cool and clear. He zipped his jacket even as he relished the pleasant evening.

Movement off to the left caught Pete's attention. He spotted someone holding a *to go* package from the restaurant that the cinema shared the parking lot with. He appeared to be headed to a car nearby. Even in the distance, Pete recognized him.

Winston.

Just as Pete bit back his surprised gasp, the man turned his head in his direction. He stopped, and his eyes narrowed. The corner of his mouth turned down in a sneer.

"You ruined my life, little faggot," Winston declared, drawing Austin's attention, who stared at him with a hard gaze. Winston's hands clenched around his keys, but he made no move to draw closer. "See you got yourself a new bodyguard."

"I didn't ruin your life, Winston," Pete countered, frowning at the clearly angry man. "I wanted nothing to do with you."

"You little liar." Winston growled the words, taking a step closer. "You wanted everything we were going to do to you and more."

"Move along, Winston," Austin ordered gruffly. "You're getting awfully close to breaking that fifty-yard limit."

Scoffing, Winston rolled a shoulder in a negligent shrug. "Whatever."

Unable to let the lie stand, Pete stated, "I never wanted anything from you or Leeson except to be left alone. Why couldn't you just do that?" Shaking his head, Pete turned to the car, finding the passenger door already open for him. "Never mind."

As Pete lowered into the seat, he heard Winston call, "You wanted it, and you know it. You shook your ass at us enough times. You'd bend over in front of us getting the mail. Hell, you practically begged us."

Austin closed the door, blocking out whatever else Winston was going to say. He shook his head as he pulled the safety strap around him. Tears of frustration burned the backs of his eyes.

Winston's words echoed in his mind even as the malice Pete had seen in his eyes sent a shiver down his spine. He just knew that if Austin hadn't of been there, Winston would have attacked — restraining order be damned. The bliss from his release was long gone to be replaced by uncertainty and fear.

What if Austin believes Winston's lies?

As soon as Austin settled behind the wheel and closed the door, Pete cried, "I didn't do that. I didn't do any of those things. I never wanted them and told them no."

Austin turned in his seat and took both of Pete's hands between his own. "I know, baby," he crooned, nodding as if to emphasize his point. "I know you didn't lead him or anyone else on."

"You do?" Pete whispered, hope fluttering within him.

Austin nodded again, his deep brown-eyed gaze holding steadily on him. "Of course, I do." Gently rubbing his wrist's pulse point, he continued, "Men like that, they're delusional. They believe what they want to believe in order to make themselves feel better about what they're doing. I know you did nothing to encourage their actions. That's all on them."

Pete let out a deep breath before forcing a tremulous smile. "I-I was worried." Repositioning one hand, he gripped Austin's back. "You're the only one I want."

A blinding grin creased Austin's goateed lips. "I've never heard anything as wonderful as that, my mate." He lifted their twined fingers to his lips and pecked a kiss to Pete's. "Let's go home. It's been a long, eventful day for both of us."

As Pete murmured, "Okay," he wondered if that had totally killed the mood between them.

After Austin had started the car and exited the parking lot, Pete asked, "Will you, will you come in with me?"

Austin glanced his way, revealing the surprise on his face. "Of course." He rested his right hand on Pete's thigh and massaged lightly. "I was hoping you'd allow me to hold you all night at the very least."

"Very least?"

Arching one dark brow, Austin glanced his way again. His lips curved into a smile that could only be called . . . wicked. "Oh, my mate. The night is still young. Do you think I can persuade you to stay awake for a couple more hours?"

Pete felt a fresh wave of arousal course through his veins. His dick, which had finally softened when facing off against Winston, began to thicken anew.

"I bet I could be persuaded."

CHAPTER NINE

As much as Austin wanted to get straight to seducing his mate, he knew that wasn't the best course of action. He didn't believe in coincidences. In his mind, there was no way Winston should have been lurking outside that restaurant, *to go* bag in hand, at the exact instant that they'd been leaving the cinema.

Even though Pete grimaced, he still nodded in agreement when Austin encouraged him to contact Detective Morrison. They once again settled in the lounge as Pete dialed the man. At the same time, Austin shot a text to Vincentius explaining what had happened.

Detective Morrison had just answered Pete's call when Vincentius strode into the room, sweatpants hanging low on his hips. Cho wore an oversized t-shirt—maybe one of the councilman's.

"Pete. Hello," Detective Morrison greeted. "I didn't expect to hear from you so soon."

"I'm sorry to disturb you so late in the evening, detective," Pete stated by way of greeting and apology.

"No, no," the detective countered. "A detective is on call pretty much twenty-four-seven, so I'm used to it. What's up?"

"I've already managed to run into Winston," Pete revealed.

"What?" the detective had a distinctive growl in his voice. "What happened?"

"Well, I went to the movies this evening with my boy-friend."

Austin couldn't help but feel his chest warm upon hearing

Pete claim him.

"Winston was in the parking lot," Pete continued. "It looked like he was leaving the restaurant that shares the parking lot with the cinema, but—"

"Right. What are the odds?" Detective Morrison asked dryly. "Did he speak to you?"

"Yes." After letting out a sigh, Pete shared what was said . . . by everyone.

"Damn it," Detective Morrison snapped. "Okay. I'm going to pass this information on to Winston's parole officer. He should be made aware of the altercation."

"He was very careful to stay at least fifty yards away," Pete continued slowly. His expression turned troubled as he added, "But there was definite malice in his eyes as he yelled at me."

"Detective Morrison," Austin cut in. "This is Austin. Pete's man."

"Austin," the detective repeated, then fell silent.

"Look, I'm in security, so I'm pretty damn good at reading people," Austin told the detective. "And this is just a gut feeling, but it's telling me that if I hadn't been there, Winston would have been more than happy to break that fifty-yard restraining order."

Detective Morrison's deep sigh came through the line. "I hear what you're saying, Austin." After a heartbeat of silence, he added, "As much as I wish I could act on gut feelings, I can't. Winston would have had to have actually crossed the line. As much as his slurs suck, freedom of speech and all that."

Austin grimaced even as he nodded. "I hear ya. I just thought I'd share."

"What I will do is pass your feelings on to his parole officer," the detective assured. "What Winston should have done was ignore you and leave the area immediately. I'll impress it upon the parole officer to remind him."

"Thank you," Austin rumbled, knowing that was the best Detective Morrison could do.

"Thank you, detective," Pete parroted.

"I'm sorry I can't do more," Detective Morrison replied. "Stay safe, Pete."

"I'll keep him safe," Austin cut in before his mate could reply.

The detective's tone sounded a little dry as he replied, "Good, but I don't want to hear about any law-breaking, either."

Austin chuckled deep in his throat. "You won't."

Detective Morrison hummed, but he didn't say more. A few seconds later, the line disconnected.

"I don't know how Winston knew that you were at a movie there," Cho began, drawing his attention. The small guinea fowl shifter was sitting on Vincentius's lap, his legs tucked under him. He held a tablet, and both he and Vincentius were studying it. "But it looks like Winston did purchase a meal at that restaurant, but his card was swiped thirty minutes before your movie let out."

"Meaning, he was waiting on me," Pete muttered, frowning.

Growling softly, Austin tightened his hold a smidge on Pete and shook his head. "He won't get you. I promise, babe."

To Austin's relief, Pete patted his hand and whispered, "I know." He smiled up at him. "I feel safe with you."

"I'm glad," Austin rumbled, pleasure flooding him. After all, it had only been that afternoon when Pete had cringed from him.

Gotta love the mate-pull.

"Well, we'll keep an eye on Winston's activities," Vincentius assured. "We'll also check to see if any of our systems have been tampered with."

"Not likely," Cho claimed with a snort.

Vincentius leveled a look full of love on his little shifter mate. "Stranger things have happened."

Frowning, Cho glanced between them. "Who bought the movie tickets? You did it online, right?"

"Um, I did," Pete confirmed. "Since Austin was paying for dinner. And yeah. Online."

Cho grimaced as he traded a look with Vincentius. The lion shifter groaned, obviously reading the look. "You don't think Winston has somehow figured out a way to track Pete's bank purchases so he can track his movements, do you?"

Shrugging, Cho told them, "One of the things that earned Winston good behavior points was vocational training while on the inside."

"Do they teach hacking in prison?" Austin asked wryly.

Snorting, Cho shook his head. "No, but if he knew a hacker on the inside, then he could get private lessons."

"Well, I guess we're hacking your bank to see if anyone else is in their system watching." Vincentius scowled as he focused on Pete. "Who do you go through again?"

After Pete told them, Cho and Vincentius rose to their feet. "We'll keep you posted." Before leaving the room, Vincentius paused and faced them again. "Maybe you should consider leaving town while we figure this out. I know Austin's vacation started today."

Austin exchanged a look with Pete, who then shook his head. "I don't want it to look like I'm running," he told the councilman. "But Austin is going to help me finish all my current work, so we can go away together next week."

Vincentius nodded. "I understand. Good night."

Austin rose to his feet and held out his hand to Pete. "Would it be okay to retire to your suite?" he asked, anticipating more alone-time with his mate.

Pete offered him a shy smile as he took Austin's hand.

"Yeah."

That smile did something to Austin's insides. It made his blood heat and his gut clench. The look was so at odds with the sexy man who'd instigated such pleasure in the movie theater. He looked forward to learning every facet of his man.

Gods, my mate is amazing.

Austin followed docilely as Pete led him down one hall and through another. He stopped at the door and gripped the knob, clearly hesitating.

Resting his free hand on Pete's back, Austin rumbled, "Nothing you don't want, my mate. Your speed. Remember?"

Pete nodded once, then opened the door. He led the way into a relaxing-looking sitting room. There was a small sofa, a recliner, an end table, and a TV hanging on the wall. There was an opening to the left, and he could make out the edge of a bed. Austin guessed the bathroom would be through there as well. To the right was a tiny kitchenette area, complete with a mini-fridge, microwave, sink, and coffee maker.

Shutting the door behind them, Pete even went so far as to lock it. When Austin arched his brow in silent question, Pete chuckled ruefully.

"This way, we won't get interrupted by well-meaning flying shifters."

"Ah." Austin nodded. "They don't always respect a closed door?"

Pete rolled his eyes as he shook his head. "Afraid not. They mean well, though."

Austin didn't bother responding. He'd heard a few tales through the grapevine about the flock living there. They'd been held and experimented on until rescued by wolf shifters and vampires. Their social skills were . . . a work in progress.

"So, uh." Pete rested his hands on his hips and glanced around. The scent of his nerves filled the room. "I'm not sure what to say." Pete faced him and shrugged. "Or what to do."

"Do?" Austin eased into Pete's personal space, sliding his

arms around him. "We don't have to *do* anything. We could just brush our teeth and curl up in bed together." With his human's nervous scent flooding his nostrils, almost hiding the smell of his arousal, Austin had to make the offer. "Is that where you want to start?"

"I-I'm not sure," Pete admitted. "I want you, Austin." Scoffing, he admitted, "I can't even describe how much I want you, but . . ." Then Pete paused, and his brows furrowed.

"But?" Austin pressed. He couldn't fix it if he didn't know the problem. Threading his fingers through Pete's tawny-colored hair, he pressed, "But what?"

Pete roved his gaze over Austin's face as if searching for something. Then he shook his head. "But, nothing," he murmured, confusing Austin even further. "I . . . I want you. Full stop. Will you bond us?"

Austin parted his lips as a surprised gasp escaped him. That certainly hadn't been what he'd expected. Unable to help himself, he had to question his mate.

"Are you certain?"

Nodding, Pete stated, "I'm certain."

"I can scent your nerves, Pete," Austin reminded him. "If you're not ready — "

Pete lifted his hand to Austin's lips, ceasing his offering. "I've watched paranormals and humans find each other and bond for several years now," he revealed as he lowered his hand to Austin's chest. "I've always wondered what that must be like. And yet, when Fate is giving it to me, I'm dragging my feet?" Pete rolled his eyes before he scoffed. "Yeah. Dumb." Grinning broadly, he ordered, "Austin, take me to bed and ravish me. Bond us. I know you want to."

Austin groaned loudly, his cock going from half-mast to aching in the blink of an eye. "Yes, I want to." Deciding to take Pete at his word, he lifted his small human into his arms.

Letting out a giggle that sounded like the most beautiful

noise in the world, Pete spread his legs and wrapped them around his waist. He twined his arms around his neck. Then he pressed a short kiss to Austin's lips before grinning at him once more.

"To the bedroom."

More than on board with that, Austin nodded. He headed to the opening, but when he rounded the corner, he stopped in his tracks. His brows shot up as he took in the scene before him.

Obviously confused as to why Austin had stopped, Pete turned to peer over his shoulder. Austin didn't make him strain himself. He pivoted so Pete would have a clear view of the room, drawing a laugh from his mate.

Rose petals were spread all over Pete's deep blue comforter. There was a bucket containing a champagne bottle on the dresser along with two flutes. A bottle of lube wrapped in a red bow stood on the nightstand.

Austin even spotted a card beside the champagne bucket, and his sharp eyesight allowed him to make out the message.

For after Austin finishes claiming you. There's also chocolate-covered strawberries and cream in your mini-fridge. Congratulations!

"Those busybodies," Pete chortled.

"Who did this?" Austin was pretty sure it hadn't been set up by Pete, considering the card and his response.

"I told you the fliers don't respect doors," Pete reminded him. Then he shrugged. "On top of that, I left Cho and Prescott in my room after dressing." When Austin frowned at him, Pete shrugged again. "They helped pick out my outfit, and I didn't want to be late, so they sorta had free rein of the place."

"Huh. Okay." Austin figured there wasn't much more to say. With a leer, he started toward the rose-petal-laden bed once more. "Let's not let all their thoughtfulness and hard work go to waste."

As Austin laid Pete in the middle of the bed, he heard his mate whisper, "Let's not. That would definitely be a shame."

Austin nodded as he whipped his shirt over his head, dropping it to the floor. "Yes, it would."

Pride flooded Austin when he spotted the appreciation in Pete's expressive brown eyes as he took in Austin's torso.

Then Austin started undressing Pete, beginning with his boots. He unzipped the side and slipped them off, one by one. Next, he eased off the man's socks, tossing them over his shoulder.

"Crunch up," Austin ordered. It took Pete a second to comply, still too fascinated with his chest. With a chuckle, Austin gripped the bottom of his shirt. "You wanna keep this in one piece?" he teased. "Or should I just rip it off you?"

"Oh, god," Pete moaned even as he lifted his torso, allowing him to pull the shirt up his body. "Another time. This is a borrowed shirt." Once his head reappeared, he admitted, "I would get no end of shit if I returned the shirt in pieces."

Barking a laugh, Austin nodded. "Well, you looked great in it."

Then Austin focused on Pete's pants, having saved the best for last. He reached for the button, recalling the feel of the silky underwear Pete had been wearing. Licking his lips, he looked forward to what he would find.

Pulling the jeans from Pete's legs, Austin revealed the sexiest pair of boy shorts he'd ever seen on a man. They hugged his mate's groin to perfection, even tented by his erection. There was even a damp spot surrounding the crown of his dick, betraying how he leaked like a sieve. Hell, that just made them sexier.

Unable to help himself, Austin pressed his face to the material. Opening his mouth, he sucked on the shaft through the fabric. He breathed noisily, reveling in the heady aroma of his aroused mate.

Austin heard Pete's cry of pleasure, felt the man buck beneath him, and gripped his hips to hold him in place. He groaned, burying his face in his human's groin, his senses singing in the best possible way.

And he knew it would only get better.

CHAPTER TEN

Pete bucked against Austin's hold, but his shifter held him steady. His gut clenched as he felt the heat of his lover's mouth through the fabric. His balls tingled, and he groaned low in his throat.

Sliding his fingers into Austin's hair, Pete relished the soft feel of the thick, dark locks. He pulled lightly, trying to get the big man's attention without hurting him. For a moment, Austin ignored him, nearly driving Pete out of his ever-loving mind by mouthing and nuzzling his dick and groin through his underwear.

God, so glad he likes them.

Finally, Austin peered up at him with heavy-lidded eyes. His arousal was etched across his features as clear as day. The need darkened his irises nearly to black.

"Get undressed," Pete urged, massaging Austin's scalp. "I need you."

That seemed to be all the urging Austin needed. He shifted his weight right and left, probably removing his shoes, while reaching for his fly. A swift move of Austin's fingers caused his heavy prick to push free.

Pete felt his eyes widen at the sight of it. For a moment, as Austin bent and shoved off his pants, it disappeared from view, but Pete knew what he'd seen. He'd felt it, but even that hadn't prepared him for the dimensions of the big man.

His chute clenched as he anticipated taking what had to be a foot-long erection deep into his body.

God, and look at how thick he is.

"Try to relax, my mate," Austin rumbled, resting one hand on Pete's ankle as he grabbed the lube with the other. "I'll take good care of you. Hurting you is the last thing I'll ever do," he assured, rubbing over his ankle. "You'll be well prepped."

Yanking his gaze from the glorious cock on display, Pete met Austin's gaze. He saw the lust in his eyes had been replaced by worry, and he knew his shifter misunderstood his fascination. While Pete knew he was a small man, he'd always loved big cocks.

I just haven't had the chance to take a real one that size.

"You're amazing," Pete murmured huskily. "I can't wait to feel you. I felt you at the movies, but . . . god, you're even better than I imagined."

Austin's eyes narrowed into a clear look of disbelief.

Smirking, Pete indicated the nightstand. "Bottom drawer, in the very back."

Cocking his head, Austin stared at him for a few seconds. Then he did as he'd been instructed. He bent, opened the drawer, and fished around a bit.

Pete did his best to fight down his flush when Austin came up with a foot-long, neon green dildo. While it didn't have quite the girth of his shifter, it definitely had the length. Austin's lips parted in obvious surprise as he met Pete's gaze.

For one heartbeat, two, Austin just stared at him. Then his lips curved into the biggest feral grin. Setting the dildo on the nightstand, Austin lifted a knee and climbed onto the bed.

"Oh, my mate," Austin purred huskily. "You are just full of surprises."

The sound of his rough chuckle caused the hairs on Pete's arms to stand on end and his nipples to bead.

"Wherever did you get a dildo that size?" As Austin asked, he gripped Pete's calves and urged him to spread wide.

Pete eagerly parted his legs, anticipation thrumming through him, causing his cock to twitch at his groin. "Special order online." That was when he realized he still wore his boy shorts. "Wait."

"Mmm-mmm," Austin countered, tracing two fingers down his silk-covered erection. "Gonna fuck you with these on. So fucking sexy."

Confused even as he was eager, Pete asked, "How?"

"Like this."

Austin reached under Pete, gripped the fabric, and rent it down the middle, exposing his hole while keeping the rest of the underwear intact.

"Oh shit," Pete whined, his body arching as not just air but Austin's finger ghosted over his hole. Panting harshly to catch his breath as he watched his lover pick up the lube, he muttered, "You ruined them."

Shaking his head, Austin smirked at him. "Improved them." Then he waggled his brows and added, "Besides, I'll get you more. Lots more."

Austin didn't give Pete time to complain again, not that he planned to. His lover's enjoyment of his underwear choice was a turn-on in and of itself. If Austin wanted to fuck him with them on, Pete was all for it.

When Austin began mouthing him through his silk shorts once more, coupled with a thick finger sliding into his ass, Pete groaned. Sparks danced along his nerve endings as his shifter easily found his gland and rubbed it gently. His gut clenched as his crown was drawn into sucking heat, even through the fabric.

The tell-tale click of the lube being opened cut through Pete's moans. "Yes," he muttered. "Oh, yes."

Austin didn't disappoint. He swiftly drizzled the cool slick onto the finger that was working in and out of his body. Pushing more and more of the lube into his body, Austin added a second finger while continuing to rub his prostate.

Pete would have felt jealous of his experience, of all those people that came before to make him so good, but he knew he was the final one. He would benefit from Austin's practice for years to come. He absently wondered just how many years that would be, since he hadn't asked Austin how old he was, and shifters could live in the neighborhood of five hundred years.

Then Austin added a third finger while pinching Pete's nipple, and all thought flew right out of his head. His balls pulled tight before he could even hope to warn the man. He unloaded in his briefs, his body jolting from the force of each shot.

Vaguely, as Pete flew on his cloud of endorphins, he realized Austin continued to suck him, perhaps drawing some of his cream through the thin underwear. His fingers continued to work him open, a fourth digit soon slipping inside him. He felt so full and so empty all at the same time.

"Please," Pete urged as soon as he could get his mouth to work. "Please fuck me."

Austin lifted his head from his groin and peered up at him with penetrating dark eyes. "Not fucking you, my mate," he rumbled gruffly. "Loving you."

Pete groaned, shuddering as his prostate was pegged once more. He didn't give a rat's ass what Austin wanted to call it. He needed his shifter in his ass . . . now.

Even blissed-out on endorphins, Pete figured that wasn't the right thing to say. After swallowing hard, he dragged a few coherent thoughts together.

Holding Austin's gaze, Pete murmured, "I need you, Austin. Please." He held out his arms and reached for his lover. "I'm ready. I promise. Make love to me." After a second more of Austin hesitating, Pete added, "Fill me with your seed and your teeth. Claim me, my mate."

Austin's features twisted into a mask of feral need as a tortured groan erupted from him. "Don't play fair."

"Not playing," Pete countered. He clenched his chute on

Austin's embedded digits. "Want you. Need you. Now, please."

Finally, Austin seemed to believe him. He gently pulled his fingers free before grabbing the slick once more. Cradling his heavy prick, he poured even more onto himself, generously slicking himself. After jacking himself a couple of times, Austin gripped his base and levered over Pete.

"Gonna make you mine now, Pete," Austin stated, his voice deep and gruff. "All mine."

"Yessss," Pete hissed, rocking into Austin's touch. He wound his arms around his shifter's wide shoulders, gripping tightly. "Want that so much."

"Me, too."

Then Austin touched his bulbous crown to Pete's hole. He pushed out as his shifter thrust. His guardian muscle relaxed, taking him in and in and in.

Pete moaned, long and low. The stretch bordered on painful, but he never wanted it to end. By the time Austin bottomed out, Pete imagined he could feel him in the back of his throat.

"Oh, fuck," Austin moaned, tucking his forehead to the crook of Pete's shoulder. "Pete, oh gods, oh mate. So good."

Feeling the big body above him tremble, Pete groaned for a new reason. He'd done that. With his body, he'd created such pleasure in him that he was racked with it.

"Austin," Pete whispered into his ear. He licked a bead of sweat from his shifter's neck before nuzzling him. "You feel so good. Fill me so full."

Austin breathed raggedly against his flesh. He slid his right arm under Pete's thigh, encouraging him to wrap it higher on his waist. Tucking his left arm under his torso, he clung tightly to him even as he kept his weight off of him.

"Feel so good, baby," Austin murmured. "Never want to move. Never want to leave." He ground his hips against

Pete's ass while muttering, "So perfect wrapped around my length. Gonna stay right here."

As hot as that sounded, Pete needed something else at that moment instead. He nipped at Austin's ear, earning a soft grunt and a moan from his lover. Then he began squeezing his chute muscles in slow rhythmic pulses.

Austin whined and shuddered once more. He trembled, whispering Pete's name as if it were a benediction.

"Move, Austin," Pete encouraged. "Make me yours. I want your seed flooding my ass."

Finally, Austin lifted his head. His eyes blazed with some kind of inner light, and Pete guessed he was looking at his shifter's animal. Gripping tightly to Austin's wide shoulder blades, he continued the massage to Austin's erection. He could see his lover's control unraveling, and he wanted that with all his heart.

Growling, Austin gave in. He peered down their bodies as he eased his cock partway out of Pete's body. Pete followed his sight and watched Austin reverse direction, sliding his heavy girth back inside him.

Austin bellowed as his control shattered. His hips sped up as he did it again and again and again, faster with each repetition. He sawed his thick cock in and out of Pete, and Pete moaned wantonly as he held on for the ride — and what a ride.

Pete clutched at his lover, reveling in the way his cock head slid over his prostate over and over. His cock ached where it was trapped within his boy shorts, but Austin didn't leave him hanging. He lowered against him, sliding against his erection with each rut.

Unable to hold back, even after his earlier orgasm, Pete felt that tell-tale tingle at the base of his spine. His balls pulled tight. He throbbed and jolted, unloading in his underwear once more as he soared on wave after wave of heady bliss.

Austin groaned his name before wrapping his jaw around

where his neck met his shoulder.

Even expecting it, the sensation of teeth popping through his flesh took Pete's breath away. He gasped upon feeling the flash of pain, but a second later, it disappeared into the sweetest ecstasy. Tingles erupted over his skin, his nipples beaded, and his gut clenched. Each suck against his neck felt like it was directly on his dick, and for the third time in such a short while, Pete tumbled over that edge, sending him into oblivion.

Feeling something warm and soft sliding over the skin of his thighs, Pete roused. He blinked open bleary eyes to find Austin staring at him with an expression that looked suspiciously like love as he cleaned his groin. His underwear had already been removed, and his lover lay naked beside him, already clean.

Pete hummed, drawing Austin's attention. The smile on his lover's face nearly took his breath away. "Hi," he murmured, for lack of anything better to say.

Austin grinned. "Hi." Then he dipped his head and pressed a soft kiss to Pete's lips. "Thank you."

Pete chuckled quietly as Austin tossed the wet cloth into the bathroom, then started using a dry one on him.

"I'm pretty sure I should be saying that to you," Pete countered, rubbing his palms over Austin's brawny arms, enjoying the flex of muscle playing under his skin as he dried him. "Never felt anything like that."

Austin hummed, his dark eyes twinkling. "Good." He threw that cloth into the bathroom, too. Pointing to the left, he winced. "We have a bit of a wet spot, but not too bad. I don't think it soaked through your comforter."

Pete shrugged as he looked that way. "It's fine. I'll toss it in the wash in the morning." He could feel his eyes growing heavy again, and he cuddled closer to Austin. "Will you stay?"

"Always, my mate," Austin purred into his ear. "Always."

"Okay."

That was the last thing he remembered before he drifted off to sleep.

CHAPTER ELEVEN

Austin had never hated mornings, but now he actually looked forward to them. Spooned up behind his mate, his softening dick still resting in Pete's chute, he relaxed with his lover. Each morning, they would lay there for several minutes, coming down from their orgasms and discussing their plans for the day.

No one had batted an eye when Austin had moved in the day following their claiming. After all, with shifters, it was damn near expected. Austin and Pete were still discussing whether or not they wanted to put his home up for sale.

"Are you looking forward to going to the cabin?" Austin asked softly as he brushed his palm down Pete's bare flank.

"Mmm-hmmm," Pete replied lazily. He peered over his shoulder at him. "A whole week with nothing to do."

With a wink, Austin teased, "Except fishing, hiking, swimming, kayaking, and rock-climbing."

Pete snickered as he rolled his eyes. He turned back around and pushed further into Austin's embrace. Austin was only too happy to tighten his grip around his warm, sexy mate.

"Do you think your brother will like me?"

Upon hearing the worry in Pete's tone, Austin nuzzled the back of his neck in reassurance. "Of course, he will." With a rough chuckle, he muttered, "I can't believe Bran's finally leaving that herd. Never thought he would."

"He's been there since birth, right?"

Austin hummed in confirmation. "Nearly two hundred and forty years." He'd shared his own age—two-hundred-sixty-two—with his mate several days before. "He's been there all this time."

"Wow."

Nodding absently, Austin couldn't have said it better. He and Bran had spoken on the phone every other day for the past week. They'd both realized it was time to put the past behind them. They were the only living relatives each other had.

What had shocked Austin was the fact that Bran had mated with a woman the alpha had chosen for him. It had ended up an unmitigated disaster. They'd ended up hating each other, and he'd never been able to get it up for her. Without children, when she'd found her fated mate, it had been easy for her to run away in the middle of the night.

Bran pretended to be nursing a broken heart for the last several years in order to keep from having his alpha force him to go through that again.

Now, it was Bran's turn to run away in the middle of the night. He intended to meet them at Austin's cabin in the woods a few days after they arrived. Once with them, Austin was going to use his connections to find a new herd for Bran somewhere close to Savannah. He already had a couple of options for his brother to review.

"I can't believe we got all caught up on the cars in time to do this," Pete mused. "You're a really good mechanic."

"Not nearly as good as you." Austin licked a stripe up the back of Pete's neck, enjoying the flavor of his human. "You even found the pinging noise in the engine on my *Stingray*. Can't believe I somehow missed that."

Pete hummed. "Glad I could help." Groaning, he eased forward, and Austin allowed him to slip from his arms. "As fun as being lazy is." Rolling to face Austin, Pete pecked a kiss to his lips. "I can't wait to get going. I haven't been to the mountains in years."

Austin kissed Pete back, then eased to a sitting position. "Then let's get rockin'." He waggled his brows as he held out his hand. "Shower with me?"

Grinning up at him, Pete took his hand. "Always."

After fifteen minutes and another orgasm each, Austin used a towel to dry his lover. He hummed appreciatively as he traced over Pete's smooth, toned form. His lover was small and compact, but so strong and resilient.

While they hadn't heard anything more on Winston, Pete never seemed to let it get to him. He kept a can of pepper spray on him at all times, although he rarely left the estate without either Austin or another shifter. It had happened only once. Pete had run to the automotive store to pick up a last-minute car part.

When Pete had returned, and Austin had realized what he'd done, he'd nearly lost his shit. Of course, then Pete had read him the riot act that he wasn't going to allow himself to become a prisoner in his own home—even if said home was a massive estate. A cage was still a cage.

Austin had known Pete was right, no matter how much him going off on his own worried him.

The make-up sex had been out of this world explosive. While Austin didn't want to fight again, he looked forward to the aftermath. They'd had to replace not only a set of sheets, but he'd needed to buy Pete two new pairs of underwear.

Leading the way to the garage, their bags in hand, they were stopped by Vincentius. He chuckled upon seeing them even as he pointed at the stuff they carried. "Are you sure you don't want to take one of my SUVs?" he asked. "How are you going to fit everything in your *Stingray*?"

Shrugging even as he shook his head, Austin claimed, "We'll play *Tetris*." Then he grinned broadly and told the councilman, "Besides. I can't wait to show Pete how much fun zipping along back roads can be."

Scoffing softly, Vincentius nodded. "Okay. Don't hit a deer or something."

"Geez, Vincentius," Pete cried in alarm. "Don't jinx us."

Vincentius lifted his hands in placation. "Sorry. Sorry." Then he waved, turning away from them. "Have a great trip. Call if you need anything. Otherwise, have a fantastic time."

"Thanks," they replied in unison, then laughed together.

Austin hurried to the garage before they were stopped by anyone else. As they carefully fitted bags into his car, he couldn't keep the smile off his face. He couldn't remember the last time he'd felt so happy.

Finally, with everything crammed into the car — sadly, Pete hadn't ended up with much leg room, but he'd assured Austin that he didn't mind — Austin brought his car to life, and they started on their way.

The drive to his mountain retreat was a little over four hours. When they stopped to fill up, Pete insisted on paying. Austin didn't want to make his mate feel bad about money, so he did his best to acquiesce graciously.

As they neared the turn-off for Austin's cabin, he admitted, "I leave a few canned goods at the cabin, since they won't attract animals, but I don't have a whole lot of variety." He pointed at the sign ahead for the small town they approached. "Would you like to stop at the market here and pick up a few things so we don't have to return to town for a couple of days?" Wincing at the bag Pete already had his feet resting on, Austin told him, "You'll have to leave it all on your lap."

Pete shrugged before smiling at him. "Let's grab a few things. I don't mind holding it." Waggling his brows, he murmured, "That way, we can run around like naked mountain men for a couple of days and won't have to come back down until after your brother arrives."

Austin barked a laugh as he turned his car into the market

parking lot. "I like the way you think."

"Knew you would," Pete teased. He hopped out of the car as soon as Austin put it in park. Lifting his arms over his head, he stretched his back. "How much farther?"

"Only about ten minutes past town." Austin found his attention snagged by the bit of skin on Pete's belly where his shirt was riding up. He felt his prick begin to fill and reached down to adjust himself. "Damn. It's gonna be a long ten minutes."

Pete met his gaze. Grinning, he laughed as he lowered his arms. He tugged his shirt down once more, then waggled his finger at him.

"Behave," Pete ordered. "Let's not traumatize the locals."

"Of course, my mate," Austin replied with a grin. Then he grabbed Pete's hand and led the way into the market. He picked up a basket and asked, "What do you want?"

Shrugging, Pete admitted, "I don't know. Do you have a grill there? An oven? A refrigerator?"

Laughing again, Austin realized he hadn't really explained about his place other than to say it was a cabin in the woods. "Yes to all of the above." As he led the way through the store, he explained, "The appliances run on propane, and I have a generator as a backup. Although I usually use the fireplace to heat the cabin."

"Toilet and shower?"

Austin grinned, amused by Pete's hopeful tone. "I can't believe you agreed to come out here even though you worried about an outhouse and washing in the river." Dipping his head, he pressed a kiss to his mate's temple. "You're so adventurous. That's just one of the things I love about you."

When Pete missed a step, Austin turned and helped steady him. "You okay?" He raked his gaze over him, then the floor, checking to see if he was injured or might have tripped over something.

"Did you just say you love me?"

Hearing Pete's soft, breathy question, Austin froze. He swiftly went over his words. Then he focused on his mate fully, offering him a soft smile.

"Not how I'd intended to tell you, but yes." Austin would never lie to his mate. "I love you, Pete. Have since damn near the first day I met you."

To Austin's pleasure, a look of abject relief warmed Pete's eyes. "Oh, good. Because I love you, too, Austin."

"Thanks be to the gods," Austin murmured.

Then, unable to help himself, right there in the middle of the store, Austin lifted Pete into his arms. He sealed his lips over his mate's and devoured his mouth. Time seemed to lose all meaning as he reveled in the taste of his human, the feel of him in his arms, and the knowledge that he was loved.

The poke of something in his leg pulled Austin out of the spectacular kiss. It was probably a good thing, since his lungs were screaming. When he broke the kiss, he panted harshly, finding Pete in the same state.

Feeling the poke again, Austin peered right and found a short old woman with a cane. For an instant, he feared he was about to get an ass reaming about either public displays or being gay or something else from a little old lady.

Then her wizened countenance creased into a wrinkly smile. "So nice to see young people so much in love. Sorry I had to break it up." She pointed at the top shelf. "Will you fetch me that box of baking mix, please, young man?"

Fighting back a laugh, Austin barely managed to keep the grin off of his face. "Of course, ma'am." He placed a heavily blushing Pete on his feet. Then he grabbed the indicated item and handed it to her.

"Thank you," she replied, placing the box in her push-cart. As she moved slowly past them, she commented, "Lube is on aisle three near the back left."

Then she rounded the corner and disappeared.

Gasping, Austin found it was his turn to blush.

Pete gaped up at him.

"Did she just?" Austin whispered.

Nodding like a bobblehead, Pete hissed, "She *did*."

Austin's mind reeled for a few seconds before he shrugged. "Better not let her knowledge go to waste." With a grin, he added, "We'll hit that aisle soon."

As Pete groaned under his breath, Austin chuckled. He grabbed his mate's hand so they could continue their shopping.

"Here we are," Austin said needlessly as he eased his *Stingray* to a stop in front of the cabin.

"Oh, wow." Pete peered through the windshield but made no move to get out. "That looks nicer than I was expecting," he admitted.

Austin tried to see it from Pete's eyes. The place was a one-bedroom, one-bath cabin. There was a large fireplace for heat. Running water came in from a spring. He'd installed a small filtration device under the sink after he'd moved in.

According to the couple he'd bought it from, they'd always brought their own water for cooking and drinking and had only used the spring water for cleaning and bathing. He hadn't wanted to go through that hassle. Austin always left the place clean with the blankets and pillows in thick plastic tubs for safe-keeping.

When Austin opened his car door but Pete made no move to get out, Austin arched a brow at him in question.

Pete grinned at him and indicated the five bags of groceries piled on and around him. "Can I get a hand?"

Oops! We may have gone a little overboard at the store. Oh well, I am a shifter, after all.

Jumping from the car, Austin hurried around the hood. He

opened the passenger door very slowly to make certain nothing was going to come tumbling out. Then he took the bags off his mate and set them on the grass. Finally, he helped Pete from his car.

After pecking a kiss to Pete's lips, Austin tugged him forward. "Come on. I'll open the place first," he told him, heading toward the door. "Then we can get everything stowed inside."

Pete chuckled, perhaps at Austin's enthusiasm. He didn't mind. It had been a good eight months since he'd been there, and he missed it. The water was calling his water buffalo's name.

After unlocking the front door, Austin led the way inside. He sniffed openly, checking for scent. To his pleasure, he didn't smell anything but stale air.

"No critters got in," Austin explained when he spotted Pete's questioning look.

"Cool."

The tour of the place didn't take long. It was pretty open concept other than the bedroom and bathroom.

"If you want to go hook up the propane, I'll start bringing everything in."

Upon hearing Pete's offer, Austin nodded. "Sounds good." He pecked another kiss to his mate's lips before moving toward the back door. He paused to open a few windows along the way to air out the place.

By the time Austin checked all the connections, turned on the propane, and had it all up and running, Pete had brought in everything. He'd piled all the food on the floor in the kitchen. The bags of clothes were in the living room.

Austin found Pete in the bedroom staring at the mattress. When he slipped his arms around his mate from behind, his lover sagged against him. Relishing the trust, Austin nuzzled his temple and cuddled him close.

Pete hummed. Turning his head, he kissed the underside of his jaw. "I was going to make the bed but wasn't certain where your stuff was." He pointed. "It's not in the closet."

"Oh, I keep it in hard plastic totes in the mudroom," Austin revealed. "Better chance it doesn't get infested with something while I'm away."

"Oh, wow. Yeah." Pete nodded. "Just show me the way. I can do that while you take care of the groceries. I figured you'd have a system I don't know."

"I wouldn't have minded wherever you put stuff," Austin told him, even though he did have a particular place for most stuff. He just would have learned where Pete wanted it.

Pete shrugged. "It doesn't matter to me, either," he said with a grin.

"Awesome." Austin turned Pete in his arms so he could kiss him properly.

Knowing they still had a few things to take care of before they began losing the light, Austin kept it far briefer than he would have preferred. Then he led the way to the mudroom and showed him the plastic bins holding the bedding and towels. After checking everything for rodents or bugs, he handed it off to Pete.

"Hey, is that a washing machine and dryer?" Pete stared at them, obviously surprised to see them.

Austin nodded. "I have a gas generator for emergencies," he explained. "They run off that. I usually only fire it up the day before I leave, wash and dry everything, then stow it away clean."

"Sounds great." Pete headed on his way.

Once Austin had brought in enough firewood for the evening as well as started a fire, he and Pete headed outside. The sun was beginning to set, but he couldn't resist a quick dip in the nearby pond.

"You're going swimming?" Pete questioned. His gaze strayed to the setting sun. "Now?"

Austin nodded. "I want to let my animal out."

Pete chuckled. "Gotcha."

Austin had introduced Pete to his water buffalo while on Vincentius's property. Unfortunately, there was no pond or lake there, so it wasn't quite the same. As he stripped, he looked forward to water play just as much as his animal.

CHAPTER TWELVE

Pete walked out the back door of the cabin and grinned. In the distance, he spotted his water buffalo wading in the pond. The big beast would occasionally dip his head in the murky depths only for it to come up with a mouthful of grasses.

Stepping off the tiny back porch, Pete strode toward his lover.

The beast stared back at him, watching him with avid interest.

Pete yanked his shirt off as he went, holding it in his hand until he neared the shore before dropping it on the ground. Then he toed off his sneakers. Starting into the water, Pete ignored the chill as he squished through the mucky bottom.

Waist-deep in water, Pete reached his water buffalo. The beast rumbled a soft grunt in hello, lowering his head and gently rubbing against him. He rubbed over the buffalo's face and horns, marveling at his lover's massive animal form.

Austin's animal stood a smidge over six feet at the shoulder. Pete guessed his heavy frame weighed in at over two thousand pounds. Austin had explained that a water buffalo could run up to thirty miles an hour to escape from predators.

As Pete watched, Austin lowered deeper into the water. Grinning, he rested his knee in the crook of Austin's horn while grabbing the upper part. He carefully clamored onto the buffalo's back.

Sprawling on the massive animal, Pete relaxed in the warm afternoon sun. His buffalo grunted softly before returning to eating.

Over the last couple of days, Pete had spent at least an hour every afternoon just like this. His lover would let his animal out to wander, and he would sunbathe on his back. His chest and arms had already begun to darken.

Other times during the day, they'd explored the area together. They'd hiked and fished along the river, bringing back a nice catch of three good-sized trout. Of course, Austin had managed to eat them mostly by himself, but Pete hadn't minded. While he'd been a good boyfriend and had tried a couple of bites, his lover knew seafood wasn't his thing. Pete had been happy to enjoy the side salad and baked potatoes instead.

They'd hiked a mountain trail together so Austin could show Pete one of his favorite views. Pete had discovered he had a bit of a fear of heights. Austin had helped him by tying them together with soft climbing rope, offering him a sense of security.

Pete had to admit, the view had been more than worth overcoming his fear.

Each night, they'd cuddled in blankets, naked before the fire. Austin would make slow, sweet love to him. They'd only made it to the bedroom one of the three nights, happy to camp out before the crackling flames.

Austin's buffalo lifted his head, drawing Pete's attention. He flicked his large ears in the direction of the cabin. Grunting softly, he began toward shore.

"You think Bran's here?"

Pete straightened on his back, straddling him. Sprawling on him while he was standing still was one thing, but he wasn't going to try it while he was moving. Hell, Pete had never even ridden a horse before.

Receiving a soft grunt in response, Pete figured that meant yes. He nibbled his bottom lip as nerves fired through him.

While he'd talked to Bran a couple of times on the phone, that was so very different than meeting in person. Pete sure hoped his being there didn't botch up his lover's reunion with his brother.

That would suck.

When they reached shore, Austin stopped. Pete carefully swung his leg over and dropped to the ground. He squeaked as he lost his balance, having missed his mark. Even as his arms pin-wheeled, Pete knew he couldn't save himself, so he let go and flopped onto the ground.

Seeing the water buffalo stare down at him with concern in his deep brown eyes, Pete chuckled. "I'm okay, big guy," he assured. "Just bruised my ego, is all."

"You're going to have more bruises than that when *I* get through with you."

Pete snapped his attention toward the cabin. Gaping like a fish, he stared as Winston stalked toward him. He had some kind of gun in hand, which he had pointed at Austin.

"Get off the ground and get over here, or I'll shoot your ugly pet," Winston snarled, wiggling his weapon.

Austin's buffalo grunted low in his throat, the noise one of unmistakable anger.

"No, don't," Pete whispered. "It's okay." He slowly rose to his feet, petting Austin's shoulder as he eased past him. "I'll be okay." Pitching his voice low, as if he were trying to soothe the buffalo, Pete mumbled, "I'll get him away from you. Then you can shift and come save me."

Even as fear permeated his body, Pete had to believe that with all his heart. His lover would fix this.

"Hurry up," Winston demanded, lifting his weapon higher. He beckoned with the fingers of his free hand.

"I'm coming," Pete responded, lifting his hands in placation. "Please don't hurt him."

"Then get over here," Winston demanded. As Pete moved toward the clearly crazy man, the guy asked, "Where's your bodyguard?"

Thinking quickly, Pete lied, "My boyfriend is fishing. Planned to catch tonight's dinner for us."

A creepy smile curved Winston's lips. "Good. It's only just past noon. That gives me plenty of time to play with you."

Pete did his best not to gag at the images that formed in his head. "How did you find me?" He'd heard somewhere that assholes liked to share their genius.

To Pete's surprise, it worked.

"Learned plenty while in prison." Smirking, Winston told him, "Not all of it legal. Like how to hack your bank information. Any time you bought something, I knew about it." With an odd sort of cackle, Winston continued. "Funny how I had to go to prison to become a criminal. Kinda like that banker in that old movie."

Pete knew which movie Winston was talking about, and he mentally disagreed with him. The banker had been wrongly accused of murdering his wife and some guy she'd been cheating on him with. Winston was an attempted rapist before he went to jail.

Yep. No correlation.

Winston lunged forward and grabbed Pete's upper arm. "Hurry up," he demanded, yanking him forward. "I got a boner that won't quit from dreamin' about what I'm gonna do to you."

When Austin grunted and lumbered a step forward, Winston once again aimed the gun at Pete's shifter.

"Wait. Wait," Pete cried, trying to ease between Austin and the gun. "Don't hurt him." He peered over his shoulder at Austin's buffalo. "It's okay, big guy. It's okay."

When Winston started to back up, taking Pete with him, Pete didn't resist. He wracked his brain for a way to stop this. If he was dragged through the kitchen, could he secure a weapon? He gave a mental groan when he realized he'd left his mace on his keychain . . . which was in the bedroom.

That would be way too close for comfort, if he ended up in there.

"See," Winston crooned, dipping his head to whisper into his ear. "Told you ya wanted my bone up your ass. That's why you're givin' it up so easy."

Yeah, no.

Still, Pete kept his mouth shut.

"Funny," a deep voice rumbled behind them. "This doesn't look like he's interested in you to me."

"What the hell?" Winston whirled, swinging his gun around.

Even before Winston had managed to get his arm all the way around, the stranger was on him. Pete dropped to the ground as the sharp crack of a gun went off. He crawled sideways, glancing everywhere.

To his right, a big man who looked a lot like Austin was easily wrestling Winston to the ground. The gun lay several feet away. Winston peered around with wild eyes even as he tried to buck the guy who could only be Bran off his back.

The man met Pete's gaze, concern glittering just a smidge within the depths of the man's hard brown eyes. "You okay, Pete?"

"Y-Yeah," Pete murmured. Just to confirm, he asked, "Bran?"

"Yep." Bran had no trouble ignoring Winston's continued attempts to get away from him as he turned his focus to Austin. "This the guy you told me about?"

Austin grunted, dipping his big head in just a smidge of a nod.

Bran narrowed his eyes, curling his lip in obvious disgust as he glanced at Winston. Clearing his expression, he focused on Austin again. "He already had his chance."

Pete didn't know if he was reminding him or Austin.

"Shifter justice?" Bran asked, his focus on his brother.

Austin grunted, lowered his head, and pawed the ground

with one huge hoof.

Bran nodded once. Then he rolled off Winston in the direction of the gun. Sweeping up the weapon, he crouched and aimed it at Winston.

With narrowed eyes and a hard expression on his clean-shaven face, Bran ordered, "Time for you to run, humie."

Even without an explanation, Pete knew Bran was insulting Winston.

When Winston lay there frozen, his gaze darting from the gun in Bran's hand to Pete to the trees and back again, Bran pointed at the sky and fired a shot.

"Go," Bran ordered again.

Winston went.

Jumping to his feet, Winston sprinted around the side of the building. When Bran just watched, Pete opened his mouth to question him. Except, an instant later, Austin barreled after Winston.

It wasn't until they'd both disappeared around the corner that Pete noticed the hand in front of his face. Looking up, he stared at Bran. While his features still appeared hard, he no longer seemed . . . lethal.

Gingerly, Pete took Bran's hand and allowed him to pull him to his feet.

A second later, the slam of a large body against metal accompanied by a scream filled the air.

Pete gasped and lunged in that direction, ready to sprint around the corner. A thick arm wrapped around his waist, stopping him. Pete wriggled and tugged, but he realized a second later that Bran had him in an uncompromising grip.

He wasn't going anywhere unless Austin's brother allowed it.

Staring up at Bran, Pete whispered, "What are you doing?"

Bran let out a low sigh as he shook his head. "Shifter justice, my brother's mate. Shifter justice." He looked toward the side of the house as more metal creaked, accompanied by other noises that Pete really didn't want to name. Without meeting his gaze, Bran continued, "It was damn obvious that if that asshole tracked you all the way out here, he wasn't going to stop until someone *made* him stop." Finally, Bran met his gaze again. "Austin wouldn't have wanted you to see that. Give him a minute to finish doing what needs doing. He'll be back in a minute."

"He's—" Pete snapped his mouth shut as realization hit. "Oh."

"Yeah," Bran confirmed. "Oh."

Pete took in a shaky breath before letting it out slowly. After nibbling his bottom lip, he murmured, "Thank you, Bran, for stopping Winston."

Easing his arm away from Pete, Bran nodded. "It was the least I could do for my big brother." He scoffed as he shook his head. Staring at the pond, his expression took on a faraway look. "After the mistakes I've made."

"But you were there when it counted, Bran," Austin stated, exiting the house. His hair was wet, and he was drying his hands on a towel. He'd slung another towel around his waist. "Thank you."

As Pete threw himself into Austin's embrace, he let out a shaky breath. His lover wrapped one arm around him, then grabbed Bran's shirt and hauled him against them both. They stood that way for a moment, and while Bran wrapped his arms around them, the tension never left his body.

Finally, Austin eased his grip. He held Bran's gaze as he stated, "Again, thank you."

Bran's features softened just a smidge more. "Happy to help."

Austin turned to Pete and gripped his ass with both hands. Lifting him against him, he stated, "Why don't you go wallow in the lake for an hour. I need to reconnect with my mate."

Snorting, Bran countered, "Tell you what. I'll give you two hours, and I'll even go clean up whatever mess you made out front first."

Grinning broadly at Bran, Austin replied, "Deal."

"That's what brothers are for," Bran countered before heading around the house.

Growling, Austin captured Pete's lips, taking him in a deep kiss.

Pete opened easily, happy to make out with Austin. He knew he wasn't the only one that needed to reconnect. He'd come so damn close to losing everything.

As Austin walked them through the cabin, Pete figured he would be embarrassed to face Bran later, but hey, that was what family was for — to help . . . and give each other a hard time.

When Austin laid Pete on the bed and stripped off his wet shorts, Pete knew he finally had it all, too — family, friends, and a future to look forward to.

Wrapping his arms around Austin's wide shoulders and his legs around his lover's thick waist, Pete vowed to cherish every minute of the gifts Fate had bestowed upon him.

ABOUT THE AUTHOR

Charlie started writing fantasy when she was eight, and after stumbling onto her first erotic romance at age nineteen, she realized her true calling. She now focuses on writing gay erotic romance, normally of the paranormal variety, with heroes of all kinds. With the help and support of her husband, Charlie finally fulfilled one of her life-long goals . . . move to acreage with her horses. You can often find her curled up with her laptop and a cup of tea or glass of wine, creating her next adventure. Charlie enjoys exploring the mountains of her new Oregon home on horseback, 4-wheeler, or motorcycle.

She can be reached at ch.richards2010@yahoo.com
Or visit her at www.charlie-richards.com.